MURDER IN SHADES
OF RED

RIPLEY HAYES

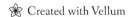 Created with Vellum

NOTE TO READERS

Trigger Warning

This book opens with a mass shooting, described in some detail. It takes place in a bookstore as a poetry reading is about to start. I understand you may not want to read about the shooting but might want to know the rest of Charlie's story. In which case, you can safely begin at Chapter Four.

ONE

SUNDAY 7PM

The gasp wrenched Charlie's attention from the podium where the MC was introducing: "Orianna Wildwood, a truly unique voice in poetry, all the way from Wales!" The air was charged with hands about to come together in welcoming applause. Orianna had taken one last drink from her gin and tonic from the temporary bar and had pushed her chair back to rise and take her place on the miniature stage. One single cry changed everything.

Charlie's head whipped round at the sound, and he saw the gunman. His vision sharpened as adrenaline surged through his body. Shock rendered the audience still and silent for a single heartbeat, and in that heartbeat only Charlie moved, *toward* the danger. Because that was the job, that was what he was trained to do, that was who he was. Instinct.

"Gun! Get down," he shouted and then he was plunging his way through the crowds and the tables toward the entrance as the man began to shoot.

"Get down, get down!" He pushed through the jungle of

people and furniture, ignoring the cries of terror and pain, and the clatter of gunfire. Adrenaline gave him strength to duck and weave, trying desperately not to be a target. He picked things off the tables: empty bottles, books, someone's handbag, and threw them at the gunman. Anything to distract him. It didn't work. The gunman was staying in the dim space where the bookshop merged into the cafe, firing in short bursts.

He's hunting.

This wasn't a random spraying of bullets; this was someone deliberately picking off individuals for death. The horror of this evil pushed bile into Charlie's throat. It also brought calm.

If he wants to shoot me, I'm dead.

Charlie was helpless to protect himself, but he would protect as many of the innocent as he could. He kept pushing forward, looking for weapons, telling people to move, get down, get away ...

Then Charlie saw the shooter for the first time as more than a shadow. A tall figure dressed in black with a balaclava showing only the white of his eyes. Eyes that realised Charlie wasn't screaming and trying to hide. The gun swiveled and Charlie threw himself to the floor, scrabbling to the nearest cover. The gunman fired a long rattling burst and dust poured from the ceiling, coating the chaos below. The gunfire stopped, and Charlie saw the man was gone. He leapt to his feet and ran through the bookshop, only to see the gunman, still wearing his balaclava, dive into a black SUV with its engine already running and speed off. There was no numberplate on the back.

Charlie ran after the car for a few yards, but it was lost, absorbed into the New York traffic, indistinguishable from hundreds of other black cars. Adrenaline washed away, leaving Charlie weary and weighed down with his own helplessness. He turned back, replaying the events in his mind, rehearsing the next steps when he heard a cry from the bookshop. A cry that cut through all the clamour.

"Charlie! Charlie! Help me!" It was Orianna. He ran back inside, ignoring the blood and the terror, the stink of human wastes and the smell of fear.

"Charlie!" This time it was a cry of agony. "Tom's bleeding and I can't make it stop."

Tom's right thigh was soaked in blood, bright red blood, blood that spurted.

Oh, fuck this is not good. Oh Jesus, Tom.

Tom was white as a sheet, sweat rolling off him, keening in pain.

Panic vied with training. Training won, but it was close.

"I've got you, Tom." *Don't fucking die.*

He ripped off his sweatshirt and then the T-shirt underneath, twisting it into a makeshift tourniquet. "We need to wrap this round his leg, above the wound," he said, as much to himself as to Orianna because he knew what he was doing, but this was Tom. *Quick. Be quick. Be quicker.*

"What should I do?"

Charlie thrust his sweatshirt into her hands. "Put this on the wound and *press hard.*" He could see the panic in her eyes and hear it in her voice and he wanted to panic along with her, because this was Tom, and Tom could die, would die, if the bleeding didn't stop. The scream rose in his throat, but he gulped it down, wriggling his T-shirt underneath Tom's leg and pulling it tight, explaining calmly to himself and Tom what he was doing, as his heart thumped loudly enough to burst from his chest.

"Stay with me, Tom," he begged. Nothing else mattered.

Then he heard the sirens from the street.

THE PARAMEDICS LOADED Tom onto a stretcher and forced a way through the aftermath like Moses parting the Red Sea, with Charlie and Orianna close behind. But the door to the bookshop was barred by a uniformed policeman.

"Please stay here, people." It wasn't a request.

"We need to go with him." Charlie heard the desperation in his own voice, felt tears rolling off his chin. "Please."

"No one leaves except the injured, sir. Please wait here."

They were trapped.

"Maybe there's something we can do to help?" Orianna took Charlie's hand.

"I need to be with Tom." But it was too late, the ambulance had gone, siren and blue lights fading into the night. Tom could die and Charlie wouldn't be there. Wouldn't even *know*.

"He's in good hands, sir," the policeman said.

"You know what? That doesn't help. Who's in charge? I saw the gunman leave in a car." The sooner Charlie got rid of the information he had, the sooner they'd let him go to be with Tom. His ribs ached with the effort of keeping his heart contained.

"I'll tell them, sir, please wait here." The cop's patience was visibly wearing thin. Voices came from behind them.

"Make way! Coming through!" Orianna pulled Charlie back as another crew of paramedics ran toward the door, one holding a drip above the injured figure, all shouting numbers to each other.

"Losing him, BP dropping fast. Go!"

Outside another ambulance waited, lights flashing, doors open.

The policeman on the door stopped anyone else leaving.

"Charlie, I want my bag, and I want to sit down."

Charlie responded to the weight of Orianna's weariness,

even as he was ready to burst out of his own skin with the need to do something, anything. He led her to a leather tub chair near the shop window.

"Wait here, and I'll get your bag." He didn't want Orianna to see any more of the carnage they had, somehow, survived.

TWO
SUNDAY 7.30PM

It was bad. There were no more screams, just crying. People clung to each other, huddled amongst the shattered furniture. Shards of glass glittered in the light where the dust had been disturbed. Charlie looked upward. The ceiling was peppered with bullet holes. Plaster dust turned the floor into a pinkish slurry of blood and spilled drinks coating every surface — including the survivors. Among the debris, two figures lay still. He didn't want to look at them, the people he hadn't been able to save. All the lights had been turned on, but the spotlight still illuminated the stage, microphone stand lying drunkenly on the floor. Charlie saw that one of the too-still figures wore the clothes of the MC and the breath caught in his throat.

Someone grabbed his arm. He turned and saw the woman Orianna had introduced earlier as: *Dana, my fixer.*

"You're Orianna's friend? Is she okay?"

"She's not injured, but she's not okay," he said. None of them were okay. None of them were going to be okay for a long time, if ever.

"What happened? How did Dusty get killed? I heard a shot, and I hid..." There was a sob in Dana's voice.

Charlie assumed Dusty was the name of the too-still figure. He thought she had been the owner of the bookshop. Her introduction had been full of excitement at introducing Orianna. He shook his head. He couldn't answer the questions.

"Orianna is sitting up at the front," he said.

"I want to stay with Dusty. I can't believe this." Dana put her face in her hands and sobbed.

Guilt vied with sorrow in Charlie's stomach, rolling around, exaggerating the stink of plaster dust, alcohol and blood. He swallowed hard. Orianna's bag was where she had stowed it out of sight. Under their table, now upturned and spattered with blood. Tom's blood. Charlie picked up the bag, and saw Tom's old leather jacket and his messenger bag on the floor. He sank to his knees, regardless of blood and dust, and buried his face in the jacket.

Tom.

The word was a scream in his head.

Pleasepleasepleaseplease.

CHARLIE RETRACED his steps through the debris toward where Orianna was waiting.

A group of women in rainbow T-shirts were huddled around a figure being tended by a paramedic. The injured woman was sitting up as the paramedic applied a bandage to her face and neck. Blood dripped from her chin, but she seemed to be forcing a smile. Charlie heard her say she was *fine* and that she hadn't been shot. The paramedic spoke quietly, reassuringly.

A middle-aged couple had their arms round each other, the woman saying: *He'll be alright. I know he will.*

Other people were crying quietly, and others sat silently, eyes unfocused. A uniformed police officer gave one young woman a blanket and spoke to her softly. Another officer had a tablet and seemed to be taking names and addresses. The man he was talking to shouted, *"You have no right to keep me here. No right."*

His companions were talking on their phones. One of them looked up and saw Charlie. His face registered horror and Charlie realised he was shirtless and covered in Tom's blood.

Two young men, college students perhaps, called to him.

"Hey, friend, thank you."

"Yes, thank you."

Charlie looked at them, not sure they were talking to him. They caught his eye and beckoned. The two were sitting huddled together next to the wall toward the front of the shop. One of the too-still figures lay in front of them, blood pooled on the floor around him. Not close enough to touch, but to move to anywhere else in the room they would have to step over the body, so Charlie understood why they stayed where they were.

"You chased that guy. Fuck, I was so scared," one of them said.

"He shot this guy, and I was sure we were next, but you chased him. You saved our lives. Jesus."

Charlie looked down at the dead man on the floor.

It was Kaylan Sully.

Kaylan Sully whom Charlie had last seen in Liverpool Prison waiting to be released into the custody of the FBI, to use his computer hacking skills for the good of his country as payback for his crimes in Llanfair. What the hell was Kaylan doing at Orianna's poetry reading? Did he know Orianna from his Llanfair days? Nothing Charlie knew about Kaylan suggested any interest in poetry. He thought back to the moments of the shooting and his certainty that the gunman was looking for targets. Had Kaylan been a target? He had been shot at close range in the chest. Had the gunman looked at Charlie after killing Kaylan and then shot up the ceiling and run? He replayed the sequence of events in his mind's eye, scanning the room for clues. This was close to where Charlie had been when the gunman caught his eye. He hadn't seen the two college students. He hadn't seen any individuals except the shooter. Everyone had been invisible as Charlie had run toward a man with a gun, trying to distract him by throwing glasses and books and even, he remembered, a chair. Because that's what had to be done.

Kaylan could have been the last person killed. Did it mean anything? He didn't know, but he thought the police should be told, because if nothing else, the shooter had murdered someone working for law enforcement.

Someone Charlie knew had been shot.

Someone *else* Charlie knew.

This is not about you, he told himself. Except at this moment, it felt like it was.

THREE

SUNDAY 10PM

After several lifetimes, someone came to talk to them. Orianna gave Charlie the spare T-shirt she kept in her bag in case she spilled something on herself before a gig. It was too small, but it didn't matter. He sat on the floor by Orianna's chair, his arms wrapped around Tom's jacket. Out of the window they saw the street fill with cars: marked NYPD cruisers, unmarked black SUVs, and a darkened van with multiple aerials sprouting from its roof. Overhead, a helicopter clattered. Men and women conferred, some in uniform, some in plain clothes, some in navy blue jackets with FBI in big letters. Floodlights illuminated the scene. The bookshop door was still blocked by the same cop who stepped aside for some, and blocked others until they argued their way past. The noise of police radios, of the cop by the door, of the sobbing from inside the bookshop blurred into a soup of nausea-inducing sound. Charlie's head was full of Tom crying in pain, and all he could feel was Orianna's hand on his shoulder and the softness of Tom's jacket in his arms.

The someone who came introduced herself as Detective Marion Levine, and she looked as sick and tired as them.

"Could you tell me what happened here?"

Charlie raised his head. She was a forty-something white woman wearing black trousers and a white blouse. She had blue gloves on her hands and a facemask pushed down onto her neck. Round her hips was a substantial belt holding a holster with the top of a handgun poking out. Her hair was thick, short and well-cut, dark, with a streak of silver in her fringe. She looked strong and competent, radiating the same kind of confidence Charlie had met in senior women officers throughout his police career. She would let him go to Tom.

"I saw the gunman. Tall, probably Caucasian. I chased him into the street. Black SUV was waiting, engine running. No license plate." All Charlie wanted to say was *I need to see Tom.*

The detective's face sharpened like a dog who has just seen a squirrel. Charlie didn't care. He felt Orianna's arms around his shoulders. She leaned forward in the chair, her breasts against his neck. It should have been comforting, but Charlie was beyond comfort. *Pleasepleasepleasepleaseplease.* His eyes were heavy with unshed tears.

"Don't cry, Charlie. He's going to be okay. He saved my life. And you saved his." Orianna's words didn't make much sense. Nothing did.

Charlie was so tired. All he wanted was to see Tom and fall asleep in his arms.

"I need to see my boyfriend, Tom Pennant. He was shot. I need to know how he is. They wouldn't let me go with him."

Levine chipped in. "If you can tell us what you saw ... police work does seem insensitive sometimes, sir, but lives might be at stake."

"Don't give me fucking *insensitive.*" Charlie's rage went from zero to sixty in less than a second. "I tried to tell your doorman what I'd seen *hours ago.* You could have had the information when it might have done some good. But it's a bit fucking late now, isn't it?"

CHARLIE FELT himself flush hot and sweaty in his anger. The outside door opened, and the cold air cooled him down too fast. His hands and jeans were covered in dried blood, and he could feel it flaking on his face. Orianna was the same. He couldn't lose the image of Tom bleeding and dying as he struggled to tie the tourniquet and stem the blood. His head swam. The shop seemed to close in around them, the bookcases looming too high and shading the lights.

"Charlie," Orianna murmured into his ear. He shook her off. Levine opened her mouth to speak, but Charlie didn't give her the chance.

"You listen to me, and then I want to see Tom. My name is Charlie Rees, Detective Sergeant Rees, Clwyd Police. In Wales. Tom and I were sitting right at the front with Orianna. I heard a noise from the back of the room, turned round and saw the gunman. About six-foot tall, skinny build. All in black wearing a balaclava with holes for his eyes and mouth. He was white — I could see a bit of skin round his mouth. I shouted to people to get down, and he started shooting."

"What sort of a gun?"

"I don't fucking know. One of those things they keep trying to ban. He was firing short bursts at specific people. Not just random shooting. Then he saw me and he shot up the ceiling and legged it. There was a car waiting for him in the street. The door must have been open, because he jumped straight in and they drove off." Charlie pointed to the right, the way back down toward Morningside Drive and into the city. "There was no license plate on the back, and the windows were tinted too much for me to see anything. The car was black, some kind of a Range Rover with lots of chrome."

"Could you identify it from a photograph?" Levine asked.

"Yes," Charlie snapped. "I haven't finished. One of the victims was Kaylan Sully. He's a criminal, a psychopath, a computer hacker and he works for the FBI." He took a breath. "He was in prison waiting to be tried for shooting me. He stole a lot of money from my boyfriend's place of work. I will give you the contact details for my boss, assuming you want them now as opposed to next week. But then I want out of here so I can go and see if my boyfriend is dead or alive."

"I'll see what I can do," Levine said. She went and conferred with one of the men in an FBI jacket who started making phone calls. "We're arranging for a police car to take you back to your accommodation," she told them, "And then you should be able to see your partner."

FOUR
SUNDAY MIDNIGHT

The bookshop was about fifteen minutes' walk from the edge-of-Harlem flat where Tom and Charlie were staying, and where Orianna had planned to spend a couple of days before heading back to the UK at the end of her book tour. The flat was the property of the arts foundation sponsoring Tom's visit and Charlie had rolled up all the annual leave he was owed, so the two of them could spend almost a month in New York. They'd been there for a week. Orianna had been doing a whistle-stop book tour around the East Coast, mostly speaking at universities. She said she had enjoyed her trip but was ready to go back to Llanfair, her job as a librarian, her wife Ann and their twins, Amelie and Ziggy. Charlie had wondered whether Tom would want to bring the girls, his biological daughters, to New York but the topic never came up. "This is for us, away from crime, and students and everything," Tom had said. That's how it had been. Lots of walking round the city, looking up at the skyscrapers, a visit to the Museum of Modern Art, and another to a piano bar Tom had been to on a previous trip. Charlie had felt the stress of his job lift as the plane left the tarmac at Heathrow. Tom had brought his work with him, or the drawing part of it anyway. The college principal part had stayed behind. Drawing was just something Tom *did*, like breathing. It simply happened. There would be a sketch pad in Tom's messenger bag along with his phone and wallet. And now ... Charlie couldn't think about it. Not until he knew Tom was okay. He wrapped Tom's jacket round his shoulders, glad of its familiar weight and the smell of leather and Tom.

An unmarked car arrived with a plain clothes driver, a tall, pale man in a crumpled suit. Outside the police cordon, the street was flooded with lights and choked with media vans trailing cables across the pavement. A few faces peered into the car as they passed but the window tint was too dark for them to see more than their own reflections. The driver tooted the horn and kept moving until the most intrusive members of the fourth estate drew away.

"I need to see you get inside safely," the driver told them when he parked by the entrance to the apartment block. The pavement was wide and tree lined, lights catching the new leaves and reflecting off the windows of their block. Orianna had fallen asleep in the short car ride, so Charlie woke her gently and helped her to the front door. The driver brought her bag. Charlie caught sight of the driver's gun as he bent over to pick the bag out of the foot well.

Lights came on in the scuffed marble-floored lift lobby, bare except for the notice advising residents about a forthcoming visit from the cockroach eradicators. Chipped marble stairs led up from the lobby, lined with wrought iron railings thick with layers of brown paint. The flat was on the top floor, so they waited for the sluggish lift to drag its doors open then make its ponderous way upward. No one spoke.

The top floor corridor was a long, thin version of the lobby downstairs. Marble floor patterned with a Greek key design and plenty of thick brown paint covering the lower half of the walls. The driver gestured for them to stay back while he examined their front door. Charlie wanted to elbow him aside and look for himself. Not that it would mean anything. He had no idea who might have a key to the block or the apartment, but he doubted that the shooter was holed up inside. He handed over the key and waited until they got the all clear. The flat was empty, quiet and still but for the hum of the huge refrigerator.

Charlie led them to the living room. One end was almost all window with views of the street trees below and more apartment blocks beyond. They must face east, Charlie thought, remembering the pale blue sky tinged with the faint pinks and yellows of dawn on his first jet-lagged morning. The walls were plain, painted cream, with a polished hardwood floor and brown aluminum window frames. He had no idea when the block had been built but the floor wasn't flat and there were cracks in most of the walls, signs of movement though hopefully not of imminent collapse.

The driver hovered by the door, showing no signs of leaving. Charlie eased Orianna onto one of three big sofas, and unfolded a blanket for her to cuddle into.

"Do you know where the injured people were taken?" Charlie looked at the driver.

"I can try to find out," he said. Then he stepped forward and held out his hand. "Brody Murphy. NYPD. Are you really a detective in England?"

"Wales." Charlie was too tired to explain that Wales and England were not the same country. "Which hospital and how do we get there?"

"Um..." Murphy pulled out his phone and rang a number.

"Can I have a look round?" Orianna asked from the sofa. "And is there anything to eat?"

Charlie showed her the three generous-sized bedrooms, the

bathroom and the miniature kitchen. Tom had turned one of the bedrooms into a workspace, pushing the bed out of the way and setting a table and chair close to the window. The sight of an open sketchbook with a drawing of himself made Charlie's heart ache, and the breath catch in his throat. He covered up by going into the kitchen for the box of doughnuts Tom kept filled in case Charlie's sugar level dropped. Or so he said.

Murphy appeared. "No word on the hospital yet. They obviously know, they're just keeping a lid on it for the media. At least that's my assumption. They're going to call me back."

"For fuck's sake. How many hospitals are there?"

Murphy went red, the flush spreading up his neck and into the buzzcut light brown hair. He looked almost as tired as Charlie felt, and as crumpled. His lightweight blue suit might have looked okay when he had left for work, but now it was dusty from the bookshop and stained with what Charlie expected was blood.

"I ... I don't know why they aren't saying," he stammered. "Sometimes the hospitals want to tell the next-of-kin before the media stake out the hospital entrance..."

The words *next-of-kin* hit Charlie like a punch to the gut. He shared Tom's house as well as his bed, but he had no official status in Tom's life. Tom had parents and siblings, as well as twin daughters. None of Tom's birth family had visited, or as far as Charlie knew, contacted Tom at all. Tom didn't complain about them, he simply behaved as if they didn't exist. All the information Charlie had about them had come from Ann, Orianna's partner, and the twins' other mother, and that was sparse enough.

They don't like that he's gay, and worse than that, they hate that he's an artist. He comes from generations of doctors. It's as if no other profession exists.

But this never-seen family would be the people empowered

to be given information and make decisions. Breathing hurt Charlie's chest.

"Have a doughnut." Orianna thrust the box at Charlie, and when he shook his head, at Murphy, who blushed again, but took a chocolate-covered ring with sprinkles. Charlie's stomach clenched.

"Which is the nearest big hospital with an emergency department?" he asked. Tom had been the first of the injured to leave the bookshop. It made sense for him to have been taken to the closest hospital. Murphy had a mouth full of doughnut and Charlie watched as he swallowed with obvious effort.

"First United, by the university. Probably."

Charlie nodded sharply. If no one would tell him where Tom was he'd have to start looking.

"I'm going out," he said. But his words were drowned by the sound of the door entry system buzzing. Murphy jumped to answer it.

"It's the FBI," he said.

FIVE
SUNDAY MIDNIGHT

Tom

Tom was floating. It should have been pleasant, but it wasn't. He could hear the calls of seabirds, the rush of waves coming in and the sucking sound of them retreating, dragging the pebbles from the beach. In, and out. In, and out. There was a sensation of sunlight beating down on his body, or was it that he could *see* the sun, because he was cold. The jingle of an ice cream van interrupted his dreams. And then shouting. He thought of families playing cricket on the beach, arguing about the rules at the tops of their voices. Surely it was too cold to play on the beach? But he could hear the waves swishing and gurgling. In, and out. In, and out.

"One, two, three. And ... thanks guys."

Tom felt hands on his body. Hands made of steel rods, sticking into him, bruising his flesh, forcing him into movement when he needed to be still. The world spun around him and when it settled his head kept spinning. There was wetness and the smell of piss. Things tore. Flesh? Clothes? Coldness against his skin and then more pulling when he needed to be *still*. Should he open his eyes? His mind told him no. The tiny part of his mind that knew this wasn't a beach; the part of his mind that dreaded this was something *much* worse than a beach, even a cold beach in winter.

"Cold," he said. Nothing changed. The waves kept going in and out. The floating feeling came back, and this time it was nice. The seabirds screamed more quietly, rhythmically, and the ice cream van's bells receded. The cricket-players must have gone for lunch because they weren't arguing, just murmuring. He floated away to the sound of the waves. In, and out. In, and out.

Charlie

The lift couldn't be heard from inside the flat so the banging at the door was shocking in the silence. Murphy went to the door, returning with two men. Both wore dark suits. Charlie wasn't sure if they had been at the scene of the shooting. Maybe it was true that everyone in the FBI looked the same. They stood in the middle of the flat's living room, dominating the space. Orianna had retreated to her spot on the sofa and Charlie felt a spike of fear from her direction, as if she was afraid these men were bringing trouble. Murphy hovered behind them in the doorway to the room, shuffling from foot to foot.

"Mr Rees, Ms Wildwood, I'm Special Agent John Mead and this is my colleague, Special Agent Andrew Bart. We're from the hate crimes team. We hope you can help us understand the terrible events of last night." If he had been at the scene, Special Agent John Mead must have made time to shower and change his clothes, which showed no sign of plaster dust or splinters of glass. Charlie was aware he was filthy with blood and dirt, and must smell of sweat and spilled alcohol but he didn't care.

Charlie held his hand up to prevent the agents beginning their questions. "I need, we both need, information about Tomos Pennant." Charlie folded his arms. Of course, they would both give all the help they could to law enforcement, but not until they knew what had happened to Tom.

"As far as I am aware," John Mead said, "all the injured were taken to First United. I have no information beyond that."

"I'll find out," Murphy said, and disappeared from view, the sound of his voice receding as he moved away from the living room. Charlie sat down on the sofa next to Orianna, and felt her hand grasp his. There was a grey space in his head where thoughts usually played and the space was full with his fear for Tom. His body was going to fall into the grey space soon. All that made up Charlie Rees would be swallowed up with terror. He was vaguely aware that the FBI agents had produced tablets and were asking if they could sit down. The voices murmured on, Orianna responding to whatever was being asked. Charlie's ears were tuned to Murphy's voice from the hallway. Abruptly, he stood up and headed out to the hall in time to hear Murphy say, "Thank you, I'll pass it on."

"What?" Charlie said. *Please don't be dead. Pleaseplease-pleaseplease.*

"Mr Pennant is in the Intensive Care Unit. He lost a lot of blood, and he's not regained consciousness. He's stable, and the surgeons have repaired the injury to his leg."

The relief left Charlie shaky, almost sick. He reached for the nearest handhold before he fainted. It was the hall table and it shifted under his weight, disorientating him even further. On wobbling legs, he led the way back into the living room and collapsed into a sofa.

"Tom is alive," he said, looking at Orianna. "He's in intensive care. I'll head over there straight away."

But Orianna didn't seem to take his words in. "These men think the gunman was trying to kill me. If Tom dies, it's my fault."

Charlie was sick with worry about Tom, and weariness weighted his bones, but he couldn't let this go.

"Orianna wasn't the target," he said looking at the FBI men, "it was Kaylan Sully. I saw it. Random shots into the crowd while he looked for a specific person. Once he'd shot that person, he quit. I didn't see the victim was Kaylan until later, but I did see how the shooter behaved. It was Kaylan they were after. He looked straight at me and shot up the ceiling as he ran off. Kaylan worked for the FBI. Surely you want to know what happened to him?"

"We'll be looking at all possibilities, Mr Rees," Mead said. "As you know, there were other people killed and injured in the incident."

"Yes. And Orianna isn't one of them. This guy shot the person in front of Ori, and the person behind her, yet here she is. If he'd wanted to kill her, he could have done. He could have killed me, but he didn't. He'd got what he came for."

"I don't suppose you have a lot of experience of mass shootings, do you, Mr Rees? Unfortunately, we do." Mead's tone was veering toward patronising.

"No, I don't. But I am a trained observer, an experienced detective, and the best witness you've got."

"Thank you for your help, Mr Rees," Mead said and stood up. He nodded to Orianna. "Ms Wildwood." Special Agent Bart stood up too, and the pair left the room. A moment later they heard the flat door bang shut.

This was all wrong. Charlie had no experience of mass shootings, but the FBI hadn't been there, and he had. He knew what he'd seen. He'd described the shooter, the getaway car and the shooter's behaviour, and law enforcement didn't appear to care. Perhaps this was a sign that he shouldn't care either, except about Tom.

Murphy cleared his throat. Charlie had forgotten he was there.

"Maybe the FBI are right," he said.

"And maybe they weren't there and I was," Charlie snapped.

"I didn't know the FBI dealt with hate crime," Orianna said, perhaps trying to pour oil on troubled waters. "I thought they did kidnappings across state lines, and serial killers."

"Those things too," Murphy answered. "Hate crime can be terrorism, so that's where they come in. Especially in shootings like this." He played about with his phone, then showed it to Orianna. It had the FBI webpage. Charlie started to look them up too, then changed his mind and put *John Mead, FBI* into the search box.

"The lying bastard," he said. "They don't give a fuck about hate crimes. Special Agent John Mead and his mate head up the cybercrimes team in New York."

SIX
MONDAY 2AM

Tom

Part of Tom's mind knew that this was a dream. The same part that told him things weren't good, that they might in fact be very bad. The part that knew he was in a hospital, though he had no idea why. So, he let the dream suppress the anxieties. It wasn't a sexy dream, but he did have his arms round Charlie as they sat on a picnic blanket in an unseasonably warm Central Park. Charlie fitted snugly against his own body. Tom remembered wanting to gather Charlie up in his arms from the first moment he caught sight of him getting drunk in the Rainbow the night before moving to Llanfair. Charlie had been drunk, and spiky, not wanting to be helped. Some of the spikiness was wearing off Tom thought in his dream, kissing the top of Charlie's head, feeling the smooth hair against his lips.

The picture changed to Charlie in the little Queer piano bar they'd been to in Greenwich Village. They'd hidden in a dark corner wanting to watch, listen to the music and drink cheap gin. A man at the next table wore make-up and a terrible wig, but he had a lovely smile and told them the history of the bar and its regulars. Tom felt the peace of the evening wash over him. Then the mood changed again. A shadow fell across their battered wooden table and Charlie was gone.

Show tunes. Songs from *West Side Story, Oklahoma,* and something about a policeman's lot not being happy. Tom smiled. He knew all about a policeman's lot. The table in front of him held drinks: gin and tonics with ice and slices of lemon, condensation running down the outside of the glasses. At the far end of the room, the bartender was singing, and to their right a man played the piano, surrounded by people belting the numbers out with big grins on their faces. A glass bowl sat on top of the piano, filled with bills of all denominations to pay the pianist. Charlie had put money in, Tom thought, but maybe he should add some more when he went to the bar.

The drinks were strong. Tom's head felt strange and a bit fuzzy. Not fuzzy enough to say no to another drink, but fuzzy enough that nothing felt completely real, as if he was looking at the scene though glass in need of a clean. A man at the next table turned to him.

"First time here?"

"No," Tom said, though his voice sounded like it was bubbling through water. "I come here when I'm in New York. I wanted to bring my boyfriend." The man nodded so hard that his head fell off. Tom leaned over, picked up the head and gave it back to its owner.

"Thanks," the man said. "Where is your boyfriend? Has he left already?"

Tom looked round and there was no sign of Charlie. But he had been there, Tom was sure.

Charlie

It was a hospital. It smelled like every hospital he'd ever been in: a mixture of disinfectant, floor polish and burned coffee. *The same, but different.* The same figures in scrubs and rubber clogs, the same people half asleep in the Emergency Department waiting room, the same noises of crying children and ringing telephones. Only the voices were different. American accents making the familiar strange. He went to the reception desk and smiled.

"I'm looking for Tomos Pennant. He was brought here after the shooting at Blue Wave Books."

Behind the desk a woman with a helmet of blonde waves smiled back, and then her expression changed to one of concern.

"Oh my, that was a terrible thing."

"I was there," Charlie said, trying to keep the smile going. "I was told Tom was brought here and I'm hoping to see him."

The woman rattled a few keys on her computer, then frowned. "He's here," she said, "but I'm afraid there's no visiting at this time, and only relatives allowed. Are you a relative, dear? From England?"

"Wales. We're both from Wales," Charlie said automatically. "I'll come back later if you tell me which ward."

"I thought Wales *was* England, and such a lovely accent. I wonder if you have access to Mr Pennant's health insurance details."

Rage rose in his throat and he wanted to grab the woman and shake her until she told him where Tom was. He forced it down and smiled again. He shouldn't have been surprised that an American hospital wanted to know who would be paying the bill.

"I have this card," he said, and handed it over. He'd extracted it from Tom's wallet, and it had the name of the insurance company and a few reference numbers. "You can see that I'm named as his emergency contact. Mr C Rees. That's me."

The woman propped the card up on her desk and started rattling her keyboard, inputting the insurance details.

"They still won't let you in unless you're a relative, but he's in Intensive Care."

Charlie managed one last smile. "I'll find it."

SHAKING legs and a buzzing in his head made sitting down an imperative. Charlie sank onto a low wall beside the main entrance and put his head between his knees, gripping the map in his hand. Rational Charlie knew that trying to operate without either sleep or food didn't work, but he couldn't face either. He would have to wait until the dizziness passed. Which it did, mostly, after a few minutes.

The map showed Intensive Care was in a different building. He looked around and saw walkways and bridges connecting the huge blocks to each other. He was attracting attention from one of the security guards, so he stood up, took a deep breath, and plunged back inside. The reception desk stood empty amid the network of corridors heading in every direction. Charlie managed to orient himself and started walking. It took fifteen minutes, two different sets of lifts, and a glass-walled bridge. Then the same glass-walled bridge in the other direction when he realised he'd taken the wrong one. He walked purposefully, as if he knew exactly where he was going and had every right to go there. No one looked at him for more than a second. The double doors to Intensive Care were locked but Charlie arrived at the exact moment a harried-looking man with a cleaner's trolley was trying to manoeuvre his way out. Charlie courteously held the door, and then slipped inside.

For the moment, the place appeared dim and deserted. There was enough light to see the bays filled with equipment, and presumably, patients. He heard voices from the far end and ducked into the first bay. Curtains were half drawn between the bays — enough that he wouldn't be spotted if he kept still and quiet. The smell of disinfectant was strong. Quiet beeps complemented the hiss of mechanically assisted breathing. The voices faded again and Charlie relaxed enough to step toward the patient just visible in the centre of all the machines, seeing a splash of dark hair against the plastic oxygen mask and the pale blue blankets. It was Tom.

Air swished in and out of the mechanical ventilator — at least that's what Charlie guessed the noise was. The beeps came from other machines with screens showing wavy lines which meant nothing to Charlie. A drip led into the back of Tom's right hand and there were so many clips and wires that Charlie hesitated to move. But he couldn't keep away. He pulled a chair close to the bed. Tom's left hand lay on top of the blanket and Charlie picked it up, whispering Tom's name. Tom's skin was warm, and the hand felt as it always did but Tom didn't stir.

"I came as soon as I could, love," Charlie whispered. "I'm so sorry." Charlie couldn't articulate why he felt responsible for Tom's injuries, but he did. He stroked the bit of Tom's cheek not covered with the breathing mask. Tears fell unseen onto the blanket and were absorbed in the waffle. "Get better, Tomos Dylan, just get better. I need you. I love you."

There was no way Charlie wasn't going to get caught but he couldn't make himself leave. The machines carried on swishing and beeping until he felt his eyelids begin to droop.

But he had run away from Tom in the bookshop to chase the gunman and Tom had almost died. Falling asleep now would be another desertion. His eyes closed, just for a minute.

Which is how the nurse found him.

Tom

Tom dreamed he was in Central Park with Charlie. He was hot, but he felt a cool breeze on his face. His sketchbook was on his lap, and his box of pencils and pastels sat on the ground next to the blanket Charlie had found in the flat. For some reason he found it hard to look down to see what he'd been drawing, but it was probably Charlie. These days he mostly drew Charlie. What had begun as a drawing and printmaking project about people and the way they lived in their homes had become a project about two men in love. Tom could draw Charlie every day and never capture his essence. *We are different people in different situations.* He had seen Charlie face down a man with a gun and not break a sweat. He had seen fiercely competent detective Charlie. He had seen nervous Charlie, afraid of saying the wrong thing to Tom's daughters. He had seen Charlie embracing art and poetry despite feeling like an imposter. He'd seen naked Charlie, so turned on that he could barely speak. And he loved all those

Charlies. Tom had seen Charlie at the Rainbow and thought him beautiful. Tom still thought him beautiful, but now he was so much more.

There was suddenly a cold sensation on his cheek and then on his forehead. Charlie must have brought some of his favourite iced coffee and be using the plastic cup to cool him down. He wanted to drink some of the awful stuff, slurp it from between the ice cubes, but when he reached for the drink, it was gone. His arm fell back against his side and wouldn't move again. Tom couldn't see Charlie in his dream, but he knew Charlie would be there. They would have a conversation about how Charlie shouldn't consume so much sugar, and Charlie would laugh and say he ran on sugar. Maybe they would decide to go for a run before it went dark... except Tom thought it was probably too hot for running, and his leg... There was an excruciating pain radiating from his right leg, consuming is body in flames of agony.

The dream began to break up. Central Park was on fire. The trees lit up like giant matches and little flames raced across the grass. Charlie had disappeared and left Tom to burn up. That wasn't right. Charlie wouldn't leave him, Tom knew that. Charlie would walk through fire to save Tom, he knew that. He'd heard Charlie's voice. All he had to do was find him.

He tried to move and screamed from the pain. He heard strange, disconnected noises: alarms, bleeps, running feet, his own voice. Someone spoke to him and the pain began to recede, leaving him floating again.

Charlie

Charlie walked back to the flat through streets which should have been empty and quiet but weren't. Sirens were almost non-stop, though always seeming to come from the next street.

There was shouting, too. Charlie only met one actual shouter: a white man in battered clothes and trainers with his feet sticking through the holes, shuffling along the pavement and cursing someone only he could see. The sun had begun to rise in a clear sky, foretelling another beautiful day. As he got closer to his destination, he was joined by a few early dog walkers. The air smelled fresh, not as fresh as at home, but not the recycled air he expected from one of the most crowded bits of the planet.

He didn't know how long he'd slept with his head on Tom's bed, but his light-headedness suggested that it hadn't been long enough. The nurse who'd found him had been alarmed at his presence, then annoyed. In the end, she had threatened him with a call to security when he refused to leave. He had begged her to look up Tom's "In Case of Emergency" contact details, but she stuck to the relatives-only line.

"So, where are these fucking relatives?" he'd asked.

"There is no need for profanity," she said, and that was the end of their conversation. He'd left without waiting for an escort from security guards, telling the nurse that he would be back. Her expression seemed to say *not on my shift, sunshine.*

The pavements were wide, and the streets wider, wide enough for double parking as well as street trees. It wasn't how Charlie had imagined Harlem when he'd heard that's where the apartment was located. The apartment blocks were often grubby from diesel fumes, but most were highly ornamented and elegant. And the flat the art foundation owned was big and full of light, far bigger than the tiny Manhattan apartments he saw on the TV and in movies. Best of all, there was a Dunkin' Donuts on the corner. In less than a week, he had eaten his way through most of the menu. Tom laughing at his sugar-and-carb addiction.

When he arrived back at his apartment block a man sat in a

parked car leaning his head against the window. It was the policeman, Brody Murphy.

Charlie knocked on the window and Murphy started into wakefulness. His face was creased from sleep, with stubble blurring his chin and cheeks. He opened the car door.

"Mr Rees. You're back."

"Have you been waiting?" Charlie asked. Murphy blushed and nodded. "Then it's a good job I woke you up." Murphy blushed harder.

"I, um, the hospital..."

Charlie decided life was too short to wait for the end of the sentence. "Lock the car and come and have some coffee."

EIGHT

MONDAY 7AM

Once upstairs, Charlie put a pod into the coffee machine for himself, and asked Murphy what he wanted. "Just black," came the reply and Charlie turned to see a sleepy Orianna peering into the tiny kitchen. She wore pyjamas made from what looked like flowered curtains, and a wrap in clashing colours.

"Where've you been?"

"To see Tom, and before you ask, all I know is that he's alive, fastened up to every machine you can imagine. They chucked me out." The image of Tom, all alone with a machine ensuring he breathed was enough to bring tears to Charlie's eyes. He blinked them back.

"We'll ring them in a bit," Orianna said.

"I didn't mean to wake you up," Charlie said, lining up a second mug.

"Can't sleep anyway. Brody has his from the red-coloured pods."

"Brody?"

"Brody Murphy. We were talking after you left."

There was the sound of a throat being cleared. "I was asked

to come and wait for you earlier, but I thought Ori ... Ms Wild-wood needed to sleep so I went and waited in the car."

Which was interesting. Not the business of going to sleep in his car, but that Murphy had been sent to wait for him. Charlie found a red pod and made the third coffee. When the liquid began to spurt from the machine, it looked exactly like his own, but perhaps there was some subtle difference he was missing. He opened the fridge. The doughnut box wasn't quite empty. He passed it to Orianna and picked up the coffees. "Let's go and sit in the living room," he said.

Orianna curled her legs underneath her on one of the sofas, balancing her drink on the arm. Charlie sat at the other end, being careful not to jolt the sofa and bring the coffee crashing to the polished floor. Murphy sat opposite them, still looking embarrassed. Orianna pushed the box of doughnuts toward Charlie.

"Eat," she said. "I don't care if it's sugar and lard, you have to eat."

Acid bubbled in Charlie's stomach, but he took a doughnut hoping it might absorb some of the acid and make him feel better. He couldn't remember a time he hadn't wanted to eat something cakey and sugary, but he had no appetite. He bit into the doughnut anyway, chewed and swallowed, feeling the hard lump make its way painfully down his throat.

"Why were you waiting for me?" he asked.

"My sergeant was concerned about Ms Wildwood," Murphy said. "And then there was a report from the hospital that someone had been seen in Mr Pennant's room. It sounded like the intruder was you, but there was a fear that Mr Pennant might be a target along with Ms Wildwood. So, that's why they sent me."

Charlie understood the individual words, but the whole made little sense.

"NYPD think Orianna was the shooter's target?" he asked.

Murphy nodded. "That's why the FBI are involved. Lots of anti-gay feeling around."

Charlie shook his head. "Not arguing about the anti-gay feelings, but that wasn't about Orianna. It was Kaylan Sully he was after, and Kaylan is dead. And that FBI guy isn't from hate crimes."

"But, Charlie," Orianna said, "Tom pushed me down when the shooting started. That's why he was shot. He was between me and the gunman." She shivered, pulling the arms of her robe down over her wrists. Charlie passed her a blanket and she spread it over her legs.

"I know you don't want to think about it but, that guy was doing two things. He was firing random shots to frighten everyone, but he was looking for someone in particular, and it wasn't you. I saw him. Kaylan was shot at close range. That's who he was looking for. Everyone else was collateral damage."

There was silence at this pronouncement.

Murphy was the first to break it. "So, who was this Kaylan?"

Charlie sighed heavily. "He was a computer hacker working for the FBI. I arrested him for conspiracy to murder back in the UK but he is such a successful hacker that the FBI brought him back. He should have been in jail. *That's* why the FBI are here. The cybercrimes FBI, not the hate crimes FBI."

"But why would Kaylan Sully be at my signing?" Orianna asked.

Charlie had no answer to that. "You haven't received any threats?" he asked, and Orianna shook her head.

"Nothing. No pickets or protests. If there has been any hate mail, no one told me about it. You could ask Dana from the publishing company. They'll know."

"It's a big jump from no contact to a mass shooting,"

Charlie said, but now it was Murphy's turn to shake his head. He put his coffee cup down on the floor.

"Those guys just turn up and let loose," he said.

"And then," Orianna said enunciating each word, "the police look at their social media. Lo and behold, it was all spelled out and no one bothered to say anything."

Murphy folded his arms across his chest.

"No one's blaming you," Orianna said.

"But maybe there is something I can do to help." Murphy looked at Orianna with something akin to adoration. She was impressive, Charlie thought, even after no sleep, wrapped in a blanket. But she hadn't been the intended victim here, and no amount of adoration would make her one. Murphy was on the wrong team in every sense.

NINE

MONDAY 8AM

"There is evidence that Ms Wildwood was on the radar of some nasty characters," Murphy said.

Orianna stared at him in horror.

"I hate to say it but here are always threats, and hate mail. It gets worse every year. Women, people of colour, disabled authors and queer authors of every kind."

"But why didn't they *tell* me?" Orianna asked.

"What good would it have done if they had? It would just make you miserable, and ninety-nine out of every hundred haters never do anything but send an anonymous email. The threats against you were generic hate-stuff. Nothing about the Blue Wave Books event."

Murphy fell silent.

"I want to see the threats," Orianna said.

"You absolutely don't," Charlie said, mentally grinding his teeth at the idea. He'd seen enough hate mail to know that reading it was a whole world of misery. He was interested to learn that Murphy *had* been aware of the threats, enough to know that the book signing wasn't mentioned.

"It might not be such a bad idea," Murphy said. "You might recognise someone or something to give us a lead."

"Or you might scare yourself shitless about nothing," Charlie retorted.

"You should get some sleep," Orianna said.

That she was right didn't help at all. And suddenly Charlie was past caring. He stumbled along the corridor to the bathroom and scrubbed himself under the shower until the blood had washed away. He wrapped himself in a towel to walk down the wonky-floored corridor to the room he had shared with Tom, dropped the towel and got under the covers. The bed smelled of Tom, and of sex, and of the doughnuts they'd shared in the middle of the night. One of Tom's shirts was draped over a chair, where he'd changed to go to the poetry reading. There was an empty coffee cup on the floor and towels hanging from hooks on the wardrobe door. The window was open letting in the noise of the street below: birdsong, shouting, music, shouting, sirens. Charlie laid his head on the pillow Tom had used and let the tears flow, and like a baby, cried himself to sleep.

CHARLIE WOKE to the same sounds from the street, and conversation from within the flat. It took him a few seconds to orient himself: the window was on the wrong side of the room and the rails of the four-poster bed loomed alarmingly above his head.

I'm in New York and I have no idea what time it is.

The conversation resolved itself into one female cut-glass voice and one generic male American one. Orianna and Brody Murphy then. His phone told him that it was four pm which didn't make a lot of sense. He was also aching and sore from having slept without moving. Worse, his heart hurt like hell because along with the realisation that he was in New York came the memory that Tom was in hospital, fastened up to machines because some bastard had shot him.

The door opened and Orianna entered with a cardboard coffee cup and a paper bag.

"Breakfast, or afternoon tea, or whatever." She put the coffee on the bedside table and looked at Charlie expectantly until he reached a hand out from under the covers to take the bag. "It's a breakfast sandwich, which is better than you expect. There are doughnuts when you've eaten it."

He put the bag, which was warm, on the bed beside him and dragged himself up against the headboard. "Thanks."

Orianna sat on the end of the bed, clearly unbothered by his nakedness. "Eat it."

Charlie opened the bag and exposed enough sandwich to take a bite. He wasn't hungry, but he would try.

"Tom?" he said when he had forced it down. "Did you ring the hospital?"

"No, but I did speak to Ann. Tom's parents should be on their way by now, kicking up a stink. He must have had them down as his next of kin somewhere. I tried the hospital, and they won't tell me anything. Brody tried too, and got the same."

He's dead. They won't talk to us because he's dead.

Charlie threw the covers aside and ran for the bathroom regardless of his lack of clothes, where he threw up the small amount of food he'd managed, retching until all that was left was bile. He rose on shaking legs and bathed his face in cold water, washing away the sweat. Orianna was waiting.

"I'm going to go there, Charlie, to the hospital. The Pennants don't like me, but when they turn up, they'll talk to me, and I'll ring you. I'm going right now, this instant, and you must drink coffee, eat something, and talk to Brody."

Sometimes, Charlie thought, the generations of army officers from whom she sprang had left their mark on Orianna. She was giving orders.

"I want to come with you."

"And I shall negotiate access. But for now, drink coffee and talk to Brody." She held her hand up to stop him speaking. "I'll ring as soon as I know anything. Tom's parents will let me in. They don't know you. They won't know you even exist. Trust me, Charlie."

CHARLIE AND BRODY MURPHY faced each other across the coffee table in the living room. The piles of hate mail were neatly stacked on the table, along with a bag of doughnuts and their two cardboard cups of coffee.

Murphy hardly looked old enough to drink, Charlie thought, let alone to have made detective. He had pale skin and freckles and large, pale blue eyes. His hair had a reddish tinge Charlie hadn't noticed before, but it went with the freckles. Charlie had no idea why Murphy was still around. So, he asked.

"I'm watching you," came the answer. "Mainly Orianna, but you too."

"Watching us? Why?"

"Because my bosses and the FBI think Orianna was the target of the shooting, and because the FBI aren't sure about your history with Kaylan Sully. Not that anyone has explicitly *said* those things you understand ..."

"My history with Kaylan?"

"He shot you. And now he's been shot."

Charlie felt his mouth drop open. He carefully put his coffee cup down on the table because the alternative would be to throw it at Murphy.

"Look," Murphy said, "it's a theory that's all. The shooting in the bookstore was chaos — you said so yourself. It's going to be a while before all the bullets are traced and accounted for. You can't deny you've got a beef with Sully, and you've been in touch with him since arriving in New York."

"No, I haven't," Charlie burst out. "The first time I saw him was in the bookshop when he was already dead."

This time it was Murphy's turn to pause. "I was told he'd met you somewhere," he said.

"Me and Kaylan, here in New York?"

"That's what I understood."

They both drank some coffee. Murphy helped himself to a doughnut and focused on eating it.

"I haven't seen Kaylan since he was in prison in the UK. I wouldn't have seen him then except we needed his help. In my head, I think of him as a psychopath, and the definition seems to fit. Believe me, he isn't someone I'd willingly spend time with. Also, if I did meet Kaylan, which I didn't, how the fuck do you know about it?"

Murphy continued to chew. When he'd finished, he licked his sugary fingers and wiped them on a paper napkin.

"I kind of want to believe you," Murphy said, "but you are obsessed with the guy."

TEN

MONDAY 5PM

"I'm not *obsessed*. I think it's likely that Kaylan was the target of the shooter, that's all. No one in law enforcement here seems to share my belief, so I'm coming to the conclusion that I'll have to do it myself." And there it was, Charlie's thoughts and intentions in two sentences. "You can help me, or you can follow me around, but I'm going to do it either way. Your choice."

Murphy didn't give a straightforward answer. Instead, he pointed at the stacks of paper on the coffee table. There were three: one twice as high as the other two put together, and one with only two sheets. "I analysed the hate mail," he said. "Bible thumpers, misogynists and this-might-be-serious. Only one of those."

Charlie picked up the two sheets of paper. The first read:

I am not afraid to kill you, Ms Wildwood. I have a gun and I know how to use it. Others may die in my attack, and you will be responsible for those deaths, too. You have a choice. Go home and sit in your library and you may live. Continue on your present course and die in a hail of bullets.

It was a copy of a letter delivered by hand to Orianna's

publisher in New York. The other was also a copy of a letter delivered the same way.

You have ignored my warning. Prepare to die.

"This is bullshit. All it proves is that someone knows Ori is a librarian, and that information isn't hard to find. If the letter writer was serious, why didn't he kill Orianna?"

"Because your Tom got in the way."

Charlie shook his head, thinking back to the carnage in the bookshop. The audience members had tried to hide under the flimsy tables, behind a bookcase, or the coffee bar. The shooter had a clear line of sight, and had been purposeful in choosing his victims, until he saw Charlie. Then he fired up at the ceiling and left. No one except Charlie posed any challenge — these were people attending a poetry reading not gangsters. The killer knew exactly where Orianna was but had run away without shooting her.

"No. He could have killed her if he wanted to. He came for someone else, or possibly he was just a nutcase who wanted to kill people. Except that if he was a nutcase, he could have killed more people and he didn't."

"Supposing you're right, how did the shooter know Kaylan was going to be at the bookstore?"

"How did you know Kaylan and I met? Even though we didn't. Which raises the question — who was following Kaylan, and who did they tell?"

Once again, Murphy changed the subject.

"So, assuming Kaylan was the target, who are the suspects? Apart from you, obviously." Murphy smiled as if to show that the last wasn't meant seriously.

Charlie leaned back on the sofa and closed his eyes. *Tom* was the first name that came to mind. Kaylan had paid back none of the money he had stolen from the art college, leaving Tom firefighting to make the books balance. If Charlie didn't know for certain that Tom was not the killer, he'd be up there on the suspects list. If Vitruvius wasn't already in prison, he'd have been on it too. Which left all the people Kaylan had met since leaving the UK. He opened his eyes and looked at Murphy.

"Off the top of my head, I don't know. I need to know what Kaylan was doing for the FBI, I want to talk to his family. I want to know who was following him." Charlie rubbed his hands over his face. Because how could he do any of that in a foreign country, with Tom in intensive care?

Why hasn't Orianna called?

"SUPPOSING I WAS GOING to help you," Murphy began, "what would you want me to do?"

"Get me access to Kaylan's flat. Find out what he was doing for the FBI."

There was a hammering at the front door of the flat. Murphy went to open the door, and Charlie wondered why whoever it was hadn't buzzed from downstairs. Special Agent John Mead appeared in the living room.

"Mr Charles Rees," he said, "we have a warrant to search this apartment, and to specifically seize your clothing for forensic examination."

ELEVEN
MONDAY 5PM

The laundry service Tom used when he was in New York had taken a week's worth of their clothes for washing the day before the shooting and delivered them back that morning. The clothes were folded then wrapped tightly in plastic bags, sealed with miles of sticky tape. The parcel of clean laundry — unopened and labelled — sat on the shoe bench by the front door. Special Agent John Mead examined the label with care and allowed Charlie to keep the contents of the package. All the rest of his clothes went into evidence bags and all Charlie got in return was a receipt. Worst of all, Mead demanded Tom's leather jacket.

"It's Tom's. The warrant says you can seize my clothes, not his." Charlie sat in his underwear on the four-poster bed, holding the jacket against his chest, while the FBI man loomed over him.

"That's the jacket you were holding on Sunday night," he said.

"It's still not mine. You want to see?" Charlie stood up and put the jacket on. The sleeves covered his hands, and the hem came below the hem of his boxer shorts.

"Nonetheless, you were holding it on the night of the shooting and could have transferred matter to it."

"*Nonetheless,*" Charlie repeated, his fists clenched inside the arms of the jacket, his blood beginning to boil, "*nonetheless,* the warrant, which I have read, thoroughly, states that you may remove *my* clothing. This jacket is patently *not* mine and you have no lawful reason to remove it." His breath came in gasps. "If you want this jacket, you need a new warrant."

"I can get one," Mead replied, his face red and his eyes wide and shining. Charlie thought he heard the other man grinding his teeth.

"Do that."

Mead turned on his heel and walked out of the bedroom leaving Charlie shaking and fighting the desire to break something. He heard the front door slam. Quieter footsteps came down the corridor and Murphy knocked on the open bedroom door.

"They've gone. Found nothing but they've turned the place over. The bad news is that they've taken all your shoes."

"Fuck! Fuck. Fuck this *fucking* noise," Charlie yelled trying to let some of the tension go. He turned round and thumped the pillows, hard. "What the fuck is going on? Why are you still here? Why hasn't Ori rung me?" He couldn't hold his anger, even as he hammered his fists into the pillows.

After a few moments, Charlie felt a gentle touch on his shoulder. He shook it off angrily, but stopped hitting the pillows. He was too tired, and suddenly too hungry. "I just don't know what's happening." His voice was weak. *I want Tom. Pleasepleasepleaseplease.*

Murphy's voice was quiet. "Phones work both ways. Ring her. If it's any help, I don't know what's happening either."

Charlie drew in a damp breath. "It doesn't help at all. But you're right about Orianna. Did those bastards leave my phone?"

Murphy produced an iPhone. "I put it in my pocket," he said. "No need to put temptation in their way."

Charlie pressed the buttons for Orianna. When she answered, she sounded breathless.

"I'm going somewhere a bit more private. Hang on." After a few moments, he heard her voice again. "He's really ill, Charlie." He heard a sob. "He's in a coma, and they're worried about infection. I don't know what any of it means except that he's really ill."

"I'm coming to the hospital," Charlie said, thinking he would go barefoot if he had to.

"They won't let you see him. Tom's parents came straight from the airport. They're letting me stay for now, but honestly, the hospital doctors want us all out of here. I think Tom's parents are being allowed in because they're both doctors."

"I'll come and wait." *Pleasepleasepleaseplease.*

"Don't. I promise I'll ring you. *I promise.* If anything happens, and if it doesn't. He's going to wake up, I know he is and when he does, I'll *make* them let you in."

"I can wait there as easily as I can wait here. I have all his insurance stuff. I'm his emergency contact." Charlie heard the stubbornness in his own voice.

"Charlie, no. You haven't met Tom's parents. They're letting me stay, but if you come, they'll probably throw us both out. They already blame me for him getting shot. You don't know what they're like. If you come here, they'll blame you as well. Please, Charlie, I'm begging you to trust me about this."

Charlie did trust her. He knew all about people who blamed him for things he couldn't control, and he was fucking *done* with it. He took a deep breath.

"Okay. I'm going to find out who did this, and then no one is going to stop me seeing Tom."

Murphy didn't say anything. Charlie could hear the hum of the fridge, and the bursts of music, shouts, and sirens from the street below. There was also birdsong. The birds must have to learn to sing extra-loud in places like this. The window behind the sofa was open a little and a breeze wafted the papers on the table. The blanket Orianna had wrapped herself in was still crumpled where she'd been sitting.

"I want to follow up that potentially genuine threat," Murphy said in the end. "I'm not saying I don't believe you, and the FBI *are* being weird, but I still want to check."

It looked like Charlie was on his own. "You do that. I'm going to find Kaylan's flat and search it, even if I have to break the door down."

"I can get the address," Murphy said. "If you tell me what shoe size you take, I'll get you some shoes. I'll even come with you. Remember I'm official."

"Won't you be too busy tracking down an anonymous letter-writer?" Charlie could hear the aggression in his voice. But Murphy didn't react.

"Not that anonymous. He's left his email address on the second one."

Charlie hadn't seen it. He rubbed his hands over his face and through his hair. He should eat. He didn't want to, but he should. He should sleep some more. What he shouldn't do was go storming off to the hospital, or to begin a completely unprofessional investigation into who the shooter was.

TWELVE

MONDAY 6PM

Brody Murphy flashed his badge at the doorman of the Upper East Side apartment block, if doorman was the right word. He buzzed them in from under the canopy covering the street entrance, into a double height marble-floored lobby with small trees in pots standing next to overstuffed sofas. A marble desk held a computer, a telephone and a number of CCTV monitors. The doorman stood up.

"Help you, officers?"

"We're here for a look round 10-F. Mr Kaylan Sully's apartment," Brody said. Charlie kept quiet. Let the doorman assume he was an NYPD officer.

"No one in," the doorman said.

"We still need to see his apartment," Murphy said. "Mr Sully is sadly deceased. Caught up in the shooting at Blue Wave Books. Can you let us in?"

"You got a warrant?"

"We don't need one. Not when the guy's been murdered."

The doorman thought for a minute and shrugged. "If he's dead, he's not going to complain, right? I can't leave the desk.

I'll get the super." He picked up the phone and a few minutes later a young Black man in navy cargo pants and a black T-shirt appeared from behind one of the trees, which presumably hid a door. He gave Murphy and Charlie a suspicious look but agreed willingly enough to escort them to Kaylan's apartment. The three of them rode up silently in the lift. A much smoother, quieter lift than the one in the apartment where Charlie was staying.

The apartment itself was everything Charlie's was not, despite being another cool and spacious three bedrooms and tiny kitchen with white walls and polished wood floors. Somehow, these wooden floors and white walls felt like luxury. Possibly because there were no undulations in either floors or walls. It also had one of the most spectacular views Charlie had ever seen, drawing him to the living room window like a moth to a flame. He had no idea which direction he was looking in, or the names of any of the buildings he could see, only that they stretched out into the distance high above the tree tops in the street below. Lights were coming on all over the city and it was magical.

"How much would a place like this cost?" he asked Murphy.

"A million bucks? More?"

The super was lurking by the apartment door. "About that," he said.

Charlie turned away from the window and sighed. "More than I'll ever be able to afford," he said. "Let's get on with it."

They started in the living room, although there was little to search. A sectional sofa sat in front of the window, and next to it, a large marble-topped dining table. A few abstract prints adorned the walls. It wasn't the room of a twenty-year-old computer genius.

"It's more like a hotel room," Charlie said, remembering

Kaylan's tiny hall of residence room in Llanfair. "Do you know if he'd been here long?"

"Coupla months. Some people buy them fully furnished," the super replied without moving from the door. "They all have cleaners anyway."

The rest of the flat was equally uninformative. A small study held a single desktop computer, and one of the bedrooms had a video-game setup but those were the only electronic devices. There was no sign of the mess of paints, canvases and sketchbooks Charlie had seen in Llanfair. There were no books. The fridge held only leftover pizza and milk. The only things out of place were a pair of tights and two pairs of women's underwear in one of the drawers in the main bedroom, suggesting that Kaylan had a regular visitor. The rest of the clothes were conservative chinos and shirts of the kind Charlie imagined would fit in with the FBI, though not with the Kaylan he knew.

"How old was this guy again?" Murphy asked.

"Twenty." Charlie was gazing around the apartment with its straight-out-of-a-magazine appearance when there was a disturbance at the door. A high-pitched female voice cried, "Where is he?"

Charlie and Murphy turned round to see the super barring the way to an elegant young woman with glossy brown hair and impossibly tight jeans. She saw them. "Who the fuck are you? What are you doing here? And where is Kaylan?"

ONCE THEY HAD SETTLED the woman into a chair at the dining table and provided a glass of water, she introduced herself as Hermione McCabe. She was a pleasant young history student, and Kaylan's sometimes girlfriend. She looked suspiciously at Murphy's NYPD badge, but Charlie's accent appeared to be reassuring.

"We weren't exclusive or anything," she said, "but he was an okay guy and ..." She blushed. "... we went to some nice places." Charlie assumed this meant Kaylan spent lots of money on their dates. "I've been calling him for days. I thought we had plans for tonight."

Charlie thought they may as well get all the information they could before breaking the bad news.

"How did you meet?"

"Some party at the university. He was doing computer science," Hermione replied. Murphy twitched at this, but got himself back under control.

"Not many students have an apartment like this," Charlie said.

Hermione raised her eyebrows. "He always said he was going to get roomies, but he didn't need to. His grandmother left him the money to buy it. He hadn't been here long. He'd been staying with his mother, but they didn't get on. I met her once, and gotta say, she is weird."

Ah, yes, the grandmother's inheritance. The same inheritance Kaylan had told Charlie he had used to pay for his sojourn in Llanfair. Either the grandmother had been richer than Croesus, or Kaylan had been up to his old tricks of diverting other people's money into his own bank account. He wondered if the FBI knew where Kaylan had been living. He also wondered if the FBI had been finding Kaylan more trouble than they'd expected. And surely his mother lived in Chicago?

"Kaylan wasn't into painting any more then?" Charlie asked.

Hermione's mouth fell open. "Painting?"

"He was studying art last year."

"He said he was doing computer science in London."

Kaylan's habit of lying hadn't changed. Perhaps it was time to tell her the truth about why they were there. Or some of it at least.

"I'm sorry to have to tell you, Ms McCabe, but Kaylan was killed in the Blue Wave Books shooting on Sunday evening."

The tears were instant. Hermione covered her face with her hands and wept. Murphy went to the kitchen and refilled the glass, bringing a few pieces of kitchen roll for Hermione to mop her face. She sobbed and snuffled for a few minutes while Charlie and Murphy sat quietly, waiting. After a while, she blew her nose, and looked up.

"I can't believe it. I lost my best friend in a school shooting, and now this." She shook her head. "I can't believe it."

Her face was red and swollen, and her eye make-up was smeared, but the weeping slowly passed. "Did you know Kaylan was intending to attend the poetry reading?" Charlie asked.

Hermione's eyes turned inward as she thought about it. "Poetry? He said he was going to see some people who could help him with something. Sorry. I can't remember much more than that. We didn't see each other that often." She blushed through the smudgy mess of her face. "We didn't talk all that much to be honest. He was kinda secretive, ya know." She took a breath. "I suggested that we go to a show last weekend, and he said he couldn't do Sunday because of these people he wanted to see. You're English, right? Why is an English person here asking questions?"

"Did he say why he wanted to see them?" Charlie asked ignoring the question about his Englishness.

Hermione frowned. "Something about how this guy had popped up in a bar in the Village, and it was weird because he needed help. Serendipity, *even if they don't think so.*" The emphasis seemed to be a direct quote.

"As if he wasn't sure these people would want to see him?"

"I guess."

Charlie asked the same questions in lots of different ways, but it was clear Hermione knew nothing more than she'd already shared. Kaylan had a problem, had met someone (singular) in a bar, and then planned to meet someone (plural) on Sunday night because he thought that he could get help with his problem. It was suggestive, but that was all. Charlie asked Hermione to look around the apartment for anything different or missing. She dutifully looked, but shook her head in each room.

"It's just like every other time I came here."

She left, and Charlie thought it was time they did the same.

"It wasn't true about the painting," a voice said, and Charlie recognised it as the super, still leaning against the doorframe. "You need to see his storage area."

THIRTEEN

MONDAY 8PM

The walk-in storage area was much more like the Kaylan Charlie remembered. As if the door had been opened and everything thrown in. Kaylan had said something like *the cleaners come on Wednesday and I'll tidy up then*. Only here no cleaners had been. All Kaylan's painting equipment: canvases, an easel, sketchbooks, rolls of brushes and boxes of paint were stacked up haphazardly on one side of the space. At some point the top items had slipped, causing a landslide. An open sketchbook lay at the bottom, stuck to the top of a jar of white paint, which had leaked onto the floor.

"I offered to clean it up," the super said, looking at the mess. "But he said not to bother. Strange guy."

Murphy picked a couple of sketchbooks from the heap and leafed through them. "He really did study painting."

"For a few months," Charlie said, "until his nature caught up with him."

"What'd he do?" The super wanted to know.

"He helped his painting tutor murder his friend," Charlie said.

"Shit," the super said. "That's harsh."

Murphy had moved on to the couple of boxes stacked on the other side of the unit. He pulled a handful of papers out of the top one, and began to read. Wordlessly he passed the papers to Charlie as he finished them.

All were printouts from news websites: The Guardian, CNN, Apple News, the BBC, the Washington Post, the North Wales Courier and Post, The Daily Mail. They appeared to have been selected at random, and stuffed into the box.

Gay Cop in Murder Trial
   Art Professor Sentenced
   Trump Will Win: Dwyer
   US Citizen Arrested after Shooting at Art School
   My Son Is Innocent!

CHARLIE READ the last one with raised eyebrows, and increasing interest.

"This one quotes Kaylan's mother. I thought she lived in Chicago," Charlie said. "When I spoke to her on the phone last year, I'm sure that's where she was. But this implies she's in New York."

"People move," Murphy replied. "Kaylan's father was shot here anyway."

Charlie whipped his head round to stare at Murphy. "What?"

Murphy handed him a printout.

CYBERSECURITY EXPERT SHOT Dead
   Roger Sully, founder of Sully Cybersecurity was fatally shot

yesterday. Witnesses say Mr Sully was about to enter a parking garage on Sixth Avenue when he was shot at close range from a moving car. The perpetrator was driving a black SUV ...

"STILL THINK THIS IS ABOUT ORIANNA?" Charlie asked.

IT WAS FULLY DARK when they left Kaylan's block. Charlie immediately rang Orianna.

"No change. The doctors are making us all leave, even Tom's folks. I'll be back at the flat in about an hour. Dunno where the senior Pennants are going, and to be honest, I don't care." Orianna sounded exhausted, and suddenly, all Charlie wanted to do was sleep. But Murphy pulled him toward the open door of a small bar, with a retro sign advertising pizza and beer. He must have sensed Charlie's reluctance because he said, "One beer, that's all."

They took stools by the bar and Murphy ordered a beer Charlie had never heard of. It came in bottles and was okay, no better, though Murphy seemed to like it. The barman poured miniature pretzels into a bowl and pushed them over. Charlie leaned his elbow on the bar and rested his head on his hand.

"What's next?" Murphy asked.

Charlie shook his head. "I need to see Tom, but Ori says they've all been chucked out. You could lend me your ID. They'd let me in with that."

"At this time of night, I doubt they'd let me in."

Charlie thought he was probably right *dammit*. And anyway, the horrible nurse from last night would remember him.

"I live with Tom, I'm on holiday with him, I'm his emergency contact and they let his parents in and send me away."

"It sucks. So, find out who shot him."

"You've changed your tune," Charlie said.

Murphy shrugged. "I still think you're wrong, but I'm not so convinced that I won't help. What do you need?"

"Kaylan's mother's address." Charlie looked at Murphy over the top of his beer bottle. "I'm not your colleague. You don't know me from Adam."

"I can tell you're a cop. Probably a good one. Come on, I'll give you a lift back."

For some reason the compliment set more alarm bells ringing in Charlie's mind than Murphy's earlier dismissals.

WHEN THEY GOT BACK to the flat, Murphy drove off, promising to text Charlie with Mrs Sully's address. The alarm bells rang again. Police officers did not help civilians with information.

Orianna was in bed, despite the early hour, but she called to him. He sat beside her as she told him about Tom.

"They think there is some kind of infection, so they're bombarding him with antibiotics," she said, not able to conceal her worry. "His vile parents were only in Boston, visiting some friends which is how they got here so quickly. And I've had a row with Ann because she gave the hospital their contact details *which she did not have to do.*"

Charlie was puzzled. What had Ann got to do with it? His confusion must have shown.

"Tom's insurance is paid for by the art college. They rang the college and got Ann because she's his secretary, and she bloody looked up his file and told the hospital how to get hold of the Pennants instead of saying you were his next of kin. For fuck's sake. They haven't seen Tom for years, but Verity is doing the whole *of course I would come to be with my darling son* routine. I hate her. If Tom were awake, he'd tell her to get stuffed."

SOMETIME IN THE middle of a sleepless night, Charlie got a text from Murphy with Sabrina Sully's address.

FOURTEEN
TUESDAY 10AM

The apartment building had the usual canopy over the entrance, and inside the outer lobby a bank of boxes with buzzers. Charlie buzzed and Sabrina Sully answered.

"My name is Charlie Rees, Mrs Sully. From Llanfair in Wales. We spoke on the telephone last year. May I come and talk to you?"

The answer came in the form of a buzzing noise, to let him through the door into the inner lobby. Unlike her son, Mrs Sully did not have the services of a doorman, though the lobby was spacious and light-filled. There were lifts on each side. Charlie studied the signs and took the right-hand lift to the fourth floor. He knocked at the door to 4A.

Sabrina Sully was tall, a couple of inches taller than him, with an athlete's physique, smooth skin and hair and an all-year-round tan. She wore white trousers and matching sweater, lifted by gold necklaces, earrings and bangles. Charlie guessed she had to be in her forties, but she could have convinced him she was thirty. Flawless grooming concealed any sign of grief.

"I am sorry for your loss," he said. From what he remembered, Mrs Sully's main interest was Kaylan and his doings. Regardless of appearances, she must be devastated. She held the apartment door open and stood back to let him in. Charlie had expected her to begin talking the second he was over the threshold but she said nothing until they reached a large L-shaped living room with modern furniture and a view of trees and sky. Glass doors opened on to a balcony, where Mrs Sully had evidently been sitting with a mug of coffee. She took her seat again, and waved him into the one opposite. She didn't offer him a drink.

"You're not what I expected. I thought British detectives wore suits. They always do on the TV."

Charlie smiled. This was more like the Mrs Sully he had spoken to last year. "Not everything is like it is on television," he said. Let her think he was there officially. In the event, it didn't matter.

"I suppose you're here about Kaylan. I really thought his troubles were over, and then to be caught in this. I can hardly believe it, to be honest. It hasn't sunk in. You know his father was killed?" She didn't wait for an answer. "I lost everything. My beautiful house, our money, our friends. If it wasn't for Andrew, I'd be going to the YMCA to exercise. My brother. He's big in the Trump campaign, you've probably heard of him. Kaylan brought all this trouble on us, but I never stopped loving him, because that's what mothers do, isn't it? They love their children and want the best for them. Obviously, I wanted Kaylan home, though there's hardly room for him in this dump. But he bought his own apartment. He has his grandmother's money; did I tell you that?"

She paused for a sip of coffee, but carried on before Charlie could speak.

"He ruined his father's business. Ruined it. Though if you asked me, which no one did, Roger should have stopped working for the Federal Government. It's too big. Americans shouldn't be paying taxes to the government. Andrew agrees with me." Another sip, but this time Charlie was ready.

"Did you see much of Kaylan when he came home?"

"Well, he came here at first. He had nowhere else to go. He was shocked of course, but it was his fault we lost the house. I thought he might offer to pay for somewhere a bit better with all his money, but he didn't. Andrew says he's self-centred and I suppose he is, but he's still my son. At least he was back here and not in that awful place."

Kaylan was in prison for very good reasons. Like shooting me, Charlie thought, but didn't say. And now whoever shot Kaylan shot Tom. He couldn't think about that now. Even though he never stopped thinking about it.

"You say Kaylan lost you the house?"

"Roger, God rest his soul, was cut out of all sorts of contracts because the government thought Kaylan would hack into their computers. Which is ridiculous. My husband ran the biggest cyber-security company on the East Coast. He had a reputation. Kaylan loved his father. He would never have done anything to hurt him."

"I thought you lived in Chicago... that the company was based there?"

Sabrina gave a tinny laugh. "Whatever gave you that idea?"

You did. When we spoke on the phone. And Chicago was Kaylan's home address when he came to the UK.

"Where was the house?"

Sabrina didn't answer. Instead, she said, "I had to identify Kaylan's body. No mother should have to do that. I had to identify my husband too." For the first time, Sabrina ran out of words.

"I was sorry to hear that your husband had died," Charlie offered.

"Immigrants," Sabrina said. "Immigrants killed my husband. I think you should go now. I've got an appointment."

"Of course," Charlie said and stood up.

As he led the way back to the front door, he took in the photographs on the wall. One was of an unmistakable Donald Trump alongside a man in golfing clothes, and next to him, Sabrina Sully. Sabrina saw him looking.

"My brother Andrew," she said, pointing at the man next to Trump."

FIFTEEN
TUESDAY SOMETIME

Tom

Charlie had spent ages looking at a Robert Rauschenburg piece made from layers of plexiglass each printed in abstract black and white patterns which played off each other depending on the angles of the light. Tom was impatient. He wanted to see the Georgia O'Keefe exhibition, and then the huge Miro in the big open space on the way out. But he told himself to get a grip. Charlie was new to all this, and he, Tom, wanted Charlie to enjoy it without feeling rushed. It wasn't as if they couldn't visit again. The Georgia O'Keefe was worth waiting for, but he struggled to focus. Paintings of desert landscapes. Hard blue skies, dark red rocks. The sun changing the colours to bronze and purple as it moved overhead, a huge yellow ball burning up the sparse vegetation, sending small animals scuttling to underground burrows, drying any moisture in an instant. Tom could feel the heat on his skin, reddening it until it was sore and peeling. He looked down at his feet. They were bare, sinking into red hot sand. The sand was blowing across the floor of the art gallery, getting deeper until he struggled to walk. The ceiling had gone, leaving only the sky and the sun and the heat, always the heat.

Tom heard himself cry out for water, but no one came. It was just him alone in the desert, sinking deeper into the hot sand, feeling his skin peeling from his body as he burned.

He heard a voice telling him there was an oasis ahead if he would just walk toward it. But when he lifted a foot out of the sand, more sand tumbled back into the hole until his foot was trapped again. He fell forward and tried to drag himself toward the oasis. It has water, and trees and soft grass the voice said. All you have to do is walk toward it.

This is a dream, he told himself. *A dream.* I went with Charlie to the Museum of Modern Art and there was no sand on the floor. We held hands and I showed him my favourite pieces, and he told me how he loved the big, crazy abstracts even though I make, and like, small, intimate prints of people. Charlie was getting the confidence to say what he liked and it just made me love him more. This is a dream of a memory, or the memory of a dream. Because it wasn't hot that day, and now he was burning up.

It's a dream.

TOM WOKE UP IN WALES. It was cold and wet as he and Charlie trudged uphill through the woods. The scent of pine trees and damp earth was strong. Lichen glowed after the rain. At the top there was a magnificent view, or there would be if the clouds lifted. On a good day it was possible to see right across the valley to the mountains of Snowdonia rising beyond. Beyond the mountains was the sea and then Ireland.

He reached for Charlie's hand, and found it slick with rain. He pulled Charlie toward him and they kissed, faces speckled with tiny drops of moisture. Charlie's lips were warm, and he smelled of sheep's wool from the new sweater he had bought from a craft stall on the market.

"It's still too warm, really," Tom heard Charlie say. "But it's cooling down. Don't you feel it cooling down?" Tom didn't know why he should worry about cooling down. He was in Wales where it rarely got hot enough to worry about overheating. Charlie would keep him warm. He slipped his hands under the bottom of Charlie's new sweater, feeling the smooth skin beneath Charlie's clothes and he kissed Charlie's neck below his ear. Breath caught in his throat and he suddenly had difficulty swallowing. Charlie was beautiful in the rain and Tom needed him so badly it hurt. He had a sudden vision of Charlie, drunk in the Rainbow, and again, in the dark outside the college asking him about his work. He licked up the side of Charlie's neck and teased the lobe of his ear, tasting the rain, and the hint of salty sweat. He shuddered with desire.

"You're tickling me." Charlie was laughing, but he didn't move away. Tom's dick was on board as Charlie pushed him against a tree and their kisses became deeper, tongues tangling. Charlie was hard too. They drew away to breathe and Charlie laughed again. "I can't get enough of you, Tomos Dylan," he said. "I even want to fuck you halfway up a mountain in the rain."

Then Tom realised that he wasn't awake. He was still dreaming. He tried to force himself to wake up but all that happened was that he was back on the path through the woods, walking upward in the mist but he was on his own. Charlie had gone. He began to sweat under his waterproofs. He wanted to take them off to cool down. He needed to wake up, but the dream wouldn't let him go. Every time he thought he was waking, he realised it was only a dream about waking from a dream.

SIXTEEN
TUESDAY NOON

Charlie sat outside a cafe not far from Sabrina Sully's apartment building, on the west side of Central Park. At the next table, a young woman was knitting and reading a book on her tablet at the same time. There was an upmarket food shop next door, and a boutique along with half a dozen cafes and bars. There were as many cars as on the east side, but it was quieter. Fewer people shouting and not so many sirens. In other circumstances, he would have been enjoying himself watching the passersby. But he needed to talk to Orianna about Tom.

"He's no better, but he's no worse either," Orianna said. "Where are you, Charlie?"

"Trying to find out who did this."

"You need to know that my fixer has been by. Dana. She's had the police round asking for all the hate mail."

"Murphy brought them over yesterday and we both looked at them. There was one that could have been genuinely scary, but the rest were getting off on writing rude words."

"You can't *know* that, Charlie."

Actually, I can, and I do. Because I was there, and because

I've been doing this job for long enough. Which is why I'm looking for who killed Kaylan Sully, and not following a dead end.

What he said was that he expected NYPD would look for the possibly genuine threat. What he thought was *why are NYPD asking for hate mail they already had?*

"But tell me more about Tom," he said.

"They're giving him massive doses of antibiotics, and I think they've hooked up even more machines. Verity sits with Tom the whole time and Gordon keeps getting all of us food and cups of coffee. I keep telling Gordon about you, but he doesn't want to hear. He says if Tom was living with someone, he'd have told his parents. Which maybe he would if they bothered to contact him. I'll keep trying. I've got photos of the two of you with A to Z on my phone. In Tom's house."

Charlie had those photographs too, and a lot more. He looked at them, filling his eyes with Tom, wishing they were warm and three dimensional, afraid that flat images would be all he had left. *Pleasepleasepleaseplease.*

Electronic noises disturbed the call.

"My boss is trying to ring me, Ori. I'd better see what he wants."

———

MAL KENT WANTED the same thing Orianna wanted — to know where Charlie was. But he asked about Tom first, and Charlie managed to tell him without letting too much of the despair come through. He hoped. Because Kent's sympathy would undo his self-control altogether.

"I'm on the west side of Central Park, sir."

"Sightseeing?"

"What's the problem?" Charlie asked. Charlie heard the

loud sigh bouncing off the satellites, or the fiberoptic cables or however the signal crossed the Atlantic. "The problem, Charlie, is the call I've just had from the New York Police Department, and the call that *my* boss had from the FBI."

Heat suffused Charlie's face. He glanced over at the woman with the knitting. He must have made some kind of noise because she was watching him with interest. He picked up his coffee cup as a distraction and took an over-hasty gulp of cold dregs.

"You are apparently interfering in an ongoing investigation into a shooting, according to my opposite number in New York, and they'd like you to stop. The FBI are investigating a hate crime and wonder why you are trying to stop them. So, inquiring minds would like to know what the bloody hell is going on."

Charlie ran through the events of Sunday night. "The New York police don't seem interested in Kaylan, and there's no real evidence that Orianna was the target. I was *there*, sir, and the shooter wasn't looking for Orianna, I'm sure of it. He had a target, and as soon as that target was dead, he fired up the ceiling and legged it. Kaylan was shot at close range. The gunman made certain. It wasn't random. And the FBI guys *say* they are looking at a hate crime, but they are actually from the cybercrimes team."

"You are interfering."

"I came here for a holiday," he said firmly. "Some bastard shot Tom and he's in intensive care and they won't let me see him. I want to know who did it."

"I expect the NYPD want to know that, too, and they have the resources to find out."

"I'm sure they do, but they're looking in the wrong place. And so are the FBI. If this was an attack on a gay writer who is also a friend, I'd hardly be opposing them. But it *wasn't*. Kaylan was the target, and my guess is that's why the FBI are interested."

"I don't know what you're not telling me. I do know this isn't your business."

"Did you know, sir, that Kaylan's father was shot in a drive-by shooting last year, and that no one has been arrested for it?"

"I didn't know, and I don't know why you think it's important. I *do* know that you are at risk of upsetting a lot of powerful people, and those people have no reason to like you. Unlike me. Time to pack it in Charlie."

There was a lot Charlie wanted to say. About how he was sure that if anyone close to Mal had been injured, Mal wouldn't rest until they were behind bars. About how the police and the FBI had everything wrong. About how an NYPD detective was *helping him investigate*. About how this *was* about Kaylan, and the more he thought about it, the more he was convinced. He didn't say any of those things.

"Listen Charlie. Reading between the lines, the FBI might not want any light shed on their decision to get Kaylan Sully out of jail. You are one of the only people who knows about what happened. It's possible they may be regretting that decision. Do you see why you might want to leave this alone?"

"Yes, sir."

"Good. I hope Tom is okay."

Charlie ended the call, and tried not to think about Tom, in a coma, without him. The only thing that made any sense at all was to keep going. He looked up to see Murphy hovering at the door to the cafe, a thick folder under his arm.

SEVENTEEN
TUESDAY 1PM

Murphy insisted on sitting as far away from the other customers as possible. "Because this is a copy of the NYPD files on Roger Sully's death, and you shouldn't be looking at it."

That meant sitting inside the coffee shop, a small, multi-level space, seeming very dark after the bright sunshine outside. They settled in a booth in the darkest corner. Murphy ordered coffee and bagels with smoked salmon and cream cheese without consulting Charlie. When the waiter left, Charlie protested and was told, "You need to eat." After that they waited in silence.

Charlie picked at his food, knowing that Murphy was right. It was only a sandwich, and starving himself wouldn't make Tom any better. After a few bites he felt actual hunger, and when the bagel was gone, the smell of warm, sugary goodness filled his nostrils.

"I'm getting a cinnamon bun," he said. "Do you want one?" Murphy nodded.

"More coffee while you're there," he said.

The cinnamon bun was perfect. The ache in Charlie's

heart hadn't gone, but he could concentrate on the file Murphy opened without his stomach growling.

Kaylan's father had died just after Kaylan himself had returned to the USA, in a drive-by shooting in the middle of the city. According to the NYPD files, the killer pointed a gun out of the window of a black SUV, tentatively identified as a Range Rover Autograph.

"That's like a regular Range Rover, but with extra chrome," Murphy told Charlie.

"That's the car the shooter at Blue Wave Books drove off in," Charlie said. "But no one seems interested in trying to find it."

"There's a note on the file saying that the DMV has been contacted for a list of all the Autographs registered locally, but there's no actual list. Also, both your shooter and Roger Sully's had no rear license plate, so the car could be from out of state."

"Still not joining the dots, then," Charlie said. "Two shootings, two black SUVs, both members of the same family."

Murphy sat back against the bench seat.

"It's suggestive, but that's all it is."

Charlie thought it was a lot more than *suggestive* but he moved on anyway.

"What do we know about Roger Sully's business? Sabrina told me it was, and I quote, *the biggest cybersecurity business in the mid-west*. But that was last year. Now she's saying that Kaylan caused them to lose all their money and that the cybersecurity company was on the East Coast. I don't get the move from Chicago to New York."

Murphy turned over some pages in the file.

"I don't know about the biggest firm in the mid-west, but they were doing well. They were — are — based in Chicago. Sully was killed on a visit to New York." He shuffled through a few more pages. "He'd come to see his brother-in-law, Andrew Dwyer."

"Sabrina implied that Dwyer was standing between her and the workhouse. Or her personal equivalent — having to use a cheap gym."

Murphy smiled. "Poor woman. Seriously, Andrew Dwyer could keep a lot of people in expensive gyms. He's a rich man. A big donor to the nuttier wing of the Republican Party. Trump supporter and proud of it."

"Kaylan said both his parents were Trump supporters, that he'd specifically chosen a college course and a teacher with diametrically opposed ideas. He was proud of upsetting them."

"That's the professor who murdered the other student?"

Charlie nodded. "Inigo Vitruvius, yes. I'll be honest, I still don't know whose idea it was to let Rico Pepperdine die — Vitruvius or Kaylan. But Vitruvius pleaded guilty to manslaughter and the FBI brought Kaylan back here and now he's dead. We should maybe look at Rico's parents, except I met them and they were just sad ... not demanding revenge. People change though."

Murphy closed the file, and put his hands on top of it.

"You can't have it both ways, Charlie. If the two shootings are connected, what reason would Rico Pepperdine's parents have for killing Roger Sully?"

Which was a reasonable question. Not that Charlie could imagine the devastated Pepperdines killing anyone.

"Anything else in the file?" Charlie asked. They were the only two people in the cafe now, and Charlie could hear the baristas teasing each other as they cleaned up their station. People were sitting outside, enjoying the sunshine. *That was me a few days ago.*

"Not really," Murphy said. "Dwyer confirmed that Roger Sully had come to New York to meet him, but declined to say anything about the subject of the meeting. Some of Sully's co-workers hinted that the company might be in trouble, which bears out your conversation with Mrs Sully. The detectives didn't appear to have any leads, and though it's still a live investigation, the reality is that it's dead."

"Hang on," Charlie said, "Roger Sully was shot heading into a multi-storey car park?"

Murphy nodded.

"Why would he have a car? He was here on a visit. There are buses and cabs and the subway, and Ubers. There's no need to have a car in the city. Surely, he didn't drive from Chicago? How long does that even take?"

"Twelve hours? Something like that. But we don't know that he had a car, only that he was going into a parking garage."

Charlie raised both eyebrows.

Murphy started leafing through the file again. "That appears to be another unanswered question," he said.

"I'd like to talk to Roger Sully's co-workers. If the firm was in trouble, is there a motive there? And did any of them know why Scully was talking to Dwyer? But I guess that means going to Chicago." Which Charlie was absolutely not going to do, not with Tom in a coma in New York.

"You might get lucky," Murphy said. He got his phone out and pulled up a screenshot. It advertised the National Cybersecurity Convention, an event happening this week in a convention centre somewhere in the city. "Want to see if we can find them?"

THE CONVENTION CENTRE was in the Bronx, not far from the Yankee Stadium. Tom and Charlie had planned to watch a game at some point, though Tom had said baseball had more impenetrable jargon than cricket and was less exciting than watching paint dry. "It's a good afternoon out, though."

Charlie watched with interest as Murphy, a supposed New York police officer, struggled to find the simple subway route to the venue. He wondered what had happened to the car.

EIGHTEEN

TUESDAY 3.30PM

Sully Cybersecurity was represented at the convention in a small stall attracting not much attention. Murphy had badged them both in. The man in the ticket booth clearly thought they were there for work and that NYPD was too mean to buy tickets. He allowed them to scan the QR code for the convention guide with obvious reluctance. According to the guide, there was a constant series of presentations, hands-on workshops and networking opportunities, and the exhibition ran all day every day of the event. The floor plan sent Charlie and Murphy away from the more crowded areas of the exhibition. A young man stood in front of the stall, looking eager. Two older men sat at the back, chatting quietly, cardboard cups of coffee in hand.

"May I help you?" the young man asked.

Murphy flashed his badge.

"I hope so. You may have heard that Kaylan Sully was killed in a mass shooting?"

The young man's eyes widened.

"Kaylan was killed?"

Murphy nodded.

"He used to be here all the time with his dad. You know his dad was murdered? Oh my gosh. Both murdered. That is scary. I thought he was in England. Oh my gosh."

This looked as if it could go on for some time.

"Is there someone we could talk to?" Charlie asked. "Whoever is in charge?"

The young man blinked and seemed to pull himself together. He turned to the two older men, who had both looked up at the Oh-My-Goshing. "Dieter? There are two detectives here to see you. About Kaylan Sully." The young man indulged in a few more rounds of "Oh my gosh," as one of the older men stood up and came over to Charlie and Murphy. His untidy hair was thick but greying, with a matching beard and skin that had spent a long time in the sun. He wore faded chinos, a washed-out Janis Joplin T-shirt and flip-flops. But his voice was educated.

"You're detectives? What's this about?"

"Could we go somewhere more private?" Charlie asked. The man led him around the back of the stall without a word, walking along a service corridor and opening the door to an empty room.

"I'm Dieter Moritz, CEO. Now tell me why you're here."

Murphy showed his badge again and introduced Charlie as a colleague. Then he told Moritz that Kaylan was involved in the shooting at the bookshop.

"Kaylan was shot? Kaylan *Sully?*"

"I'm sorry to have to tell you that he died. My colleague here has spoken to Mrs Sully, and she holds Kaylan responsible for the decline of this company. That, and the death of her husband. I wanted to see if there was any truth in what she told me."

Moritz looked stunned; his eyes as wide as the young man's.

"Sir," said Charlie, "can I get you a glass of water?"

Moritz shook his head, bringing his eyes back into focus on Charlie.

"I'm fine." A pause. "Shit. I hated that boy and all his schemes, but I wouldn't see him dead. Shit."

Charlie thought this was the equivalent of the receptionist's oh-my-goshing, but it didn't last.

"Mrs Sully told it right. There were four hundred people employed until the word started to spread about Kaylan stealing money from his high school. Chicago might look like a big city and a lot of people trusted us to keep their data safe. Thing is, they all talk to each other. One of our clients was the Cook County Department of Education. Our reputation was word of mouth, and that works in two directions."

"Mrs Sully said you lost federal contracts."

Moritz snorted. "Those bastards just wanted an excuse to dump us. Dwyer and his cronies shouting about big government robbing the American taxpayer, then lobbying to shovel federal money toward his brother-in-law's firm. The Dems just took their opportunity to badmouth us and shovel the money to their cronies." He shrugged. "But we were doing good work. Those jobs meant people had healthcare and paid taxes." Moritz dragged his hand over his face and beard. "You know, Dwyer lost his brother-in-law and now his nephew to gun crime, and he still thinks gun control is the work of the devil. The whole family is gun-mad. This country is crazy."

A lot of people had cause to dislike Kaylan Sully, but as far as Charlie could tell, they were nowhere near the bookshop when he was killed. Moritz didn't appear to have anything else to say.

"Go and have a look round," he said to Murphy. "I'm going to wait outside for a bit."

"I'll come with you," Murphy said.

Charlie gave him a sharp look. "Don't get in the way," he

snapped. He found a seat on a bench just outside the main entrance to the convention. Murphy sat two benches away and started scrolling through his phone.

Maybe he was wasting his time. But he didn't move from the bench, and after what seemed like several hours, but was probably about twenty minutes, the young man came out, and he was alone. Charlie stood up.

"Hi," he said. "Can I buy you a coffee? Or a drink?"

The young man looked Charlie up and down. "Only if you tell me what you expect to get out of it."

"Information," Charlie said with a smile.

"Coffee then. And my name is Evan."

"Charlie."

Evan ducked into a narrow alley between two buildings, next to the convention centre. At the end, a rainbow flag hung over the door to the Hidden Bean Cafe. The space was small and the smell of the coffee was seductive. A glass display unit offered a selection of cakes, variously labelled with their ingredients and potential allergens and Charlie felt the familiar desire for sugar. He ordered coffee and a brownie and a green tea for Evan. No cake. He suddenly had a powerful desire to be back in the police station in Llanfair, listening to Eddy and Patsy squabble about whose turn it was to go and get more supplies of chocolate. He swallowed the feeling and realised Evan was looking at him expectantly.

"What information do you want?" he asked.

"Do you work for Sully Cybersecurity full time?"

Evan nodded. "I've been there for the last three years. They don't mind me studying when it isn't busy. Which is most of the time now. I'm not sure how much longer they can keep going to be honest."

"And this is all down to word getting out about Kaylan's hacking habits?"

"Mostly. Everything got worse when Roger Sully was killed. It was his company. Dieter's a nice guy, but Roger was absolutely driven. Always out making contacts, going to DC, New York, the West Coast and he loved a gun show. Roger picked up jobs from their political friends and the gun lobby. Dieter doesn't have those contacts, though he does try. Also, he's in favour of gun control and he might even be a Democrat."

"But he's the new CEO?"

"I know, right? Thing is, most people just want to do the computer stuff and they don't care who it's for — the federal government or the Trump campaign."

"So," Charlie asked, "you've got all these people who love guns working for a company that Kaylan Sully almost destroyed..."

The shock on Evan's face was a picture. "Oh my gosh. Oh my gosh. That's..." The shock faded to be replaced by something more thoughtful. "No one would do that." But the denial wasn't convincing.

"Someone did."

"I have to go." Evan scrambled to his feet and almost ran out of the cafe.

Charlie finished his brownie and thought about what to do next.

NINETEEN

Murphy was standing by the door to the cafe and Charlie went to join him. The sunshine from earlier had changed to cloudy skies, and it was heavily shaded in the alley as they walked back to the street, Charlie sharing what he'd learned from Evan. The end of the alley was blocked by a brown delivery van with a couple of big guys moving boxes. As Charlie stepped to go round the back of the van, he felt himself lifted off his feet by heavily muscled arms grabbing his own. Shock stopped him for a breath then he opened his mouth to yell. Something jabbed into his side, and a big hand in a leather glove covered his mouth and nose. Charlie thrashed, looking around wildly for Brody Murphy. But Murphy had disappeared as if he had never been there.

"Keep quiet, asshole," a voice said. Charlie had no choice but to comply because he couldn't breathe. He was half thrown into the back of the van, managing to land on his knees and opening his mouth to yell again. But it was too late. The door was closed and the van was moving. He moved to bang on the side of the van, but the man in the leather gloves moved faster and hit him in the stomach. Charlie fell back against a pile of cardboard and gasped for breath. The pain was as bad as when he'd been shot.

"I said, be quiet,"

All Charlie could do was attempt to drag air into his lungs and wait for the pain to pass. When he looked up, still wheezing, he saw the second man holding a handgun very steadily, pointed directly at him. The van was an empty metal box with windows in the roof, but not in the sides, and no indication of what it might be used to deliver.

"What's going on?" Charlie stammered.

"What part of *shut the fuck up* are you not understanding?" the man with the gun growled.

Charlie knew if he was going to get out of this, he needed all his strength. Another blow from leather-gloves-man would make things worse. He kept quiet. The two men said nothing and their watch on him never wavered. They wore jeans, sweatshirts and baseball caps with heavy boots. Both were short and broad with plenty of obvious muscle — they had picked him up as if he weighed nothing. They could have been brothers, both white men with dark curly hair and goatees and Charlie thought they still seemed more like a pair of delivery drivers than the thugs they were. There was a panel dividing the front and back of the van so Charlie had no idea who was driving. But he would remember these two faces — if he got the chance.

The van moved steadily, stopping and starting, turning corners, and occasionally speeding up, though not much. Charlie heard the New York traffic all around them: horns, blasts of music and the ubiquitous sirens. A few minutes into the drive, outside noises lessened, and a few minutes after that, stopped altogether.

The back door opened and the man with gun gestured for

Charlie to move. This would be his chance to get away. Except these guys had done this before. As Charlie stepped toward the door, leather-gloves-man grabbed his arm with fingers like a mechanical grabber and the other man jabbed the gun into Charlie's kidneys. They exited the van, Charlie stumbling, keeping his balance with difficulty. They were in the middle of a construction site on an almost empty flattened-rubble car park next to a block of temporary offices and containers. What Charlie guessed was a concrete mixing plant stood next to a high wooden fence. More high fencing cut them off from the street. Traffic thundered on an elevated street almost overhead. The smell of diesel fumes and construction dust filled the air.

A door in the site offices opened and a man of Charlie's height with a substantial gut appeared.

"This him? I was expecting something a bit more impressive, gotta say."

This from a man who looked like a garden gnome and supported Donald Trump.

Charlie recognised Andrew Dwyer from the photographs in Sabrina Sully's home. "Don't bother to speak, Mr Rees," Dwyer said. "What I've got to say won't take long and then we can all get on with our day."

Charlie stood and said nothing.

"My nephew Kaylan was a much-misunderstood young man. He was murdered by someone who came to kill your dyke friend. You are in no position to try to tarnish his reputation, not with your history. I don't like your sort, Mr Rees. You're away from home and you've got no friends here. Fuck off and forget about Kaylan. I don't want to see your face or hear your name again. Okay?"

Charlie said nothing, which was apparently the wrong thing to do. He got another jab in the kidneys from the man with the gun. But they hadn't brought him here to kill him, just to warn him off. Relief and confidence washed over him like water.

"I'm a British police officer, Mr Dwyer," he began. Dwyer took a step forward and hit Charlie across the face so hard that he rocked back on his heels, only staying upright because of leather-gloves-man's grip on his arm.

"I know what you are," he said and hit Charlie again. Charlie felt blood in his mouth, and the sharpness of pain inside his cheek. "Don't make me change my mind about letting you go." He nodded at the two thugs and went back into the office.

Charlie was unceremoniously bundled back into the van. The door closed and the van started to move. They drove for what could have been about ten minutes, though Charlie's head was spinning so badly that he had little sense of time. The van stopped and the door opened. Leather-gloves-man pulled Charlie to the door and pushed. The impact with the pavement was brutal, jarring every bone in his body. The ground scraped his hands and knees like it was made of rough sandpaper. He bit his cheek and felt his mouth fill with blood again. Charlie could do nothing but watch as the door closed and the van drove off. There was no numberplate. Charlie was getting tired of the whole no-numberplate thing.

Then it started to rain.

TWENTY
TUESDAY 7PM

Tom

There was something familiar about the young man. Tom thought he might be one of his students, though why one of his students would be here, in a piano bar in New York, Tom didn't know. The edges of the bar had gone fuzzy. It was all still there, he knew that, he just couldn't quite see it. The young man was talking to him, holding Tom's arm, and speaking rapidly into Tom's ear. Something about his mother. Did Tom care about this boy's mother? He thought he was probably expected to care because he was in charge of all the students.

"This is a dream. It isn't real."

Who said that? Charlie? "My mother is calling. I'd better go and talk to her."

Tom thought he heard his own mother, but it was a dream. It wasn't real. He hadn't seen his mother for years. She didn't like him.

The young man's face swam into Tom's view, looming larger and larger until it filled the screen. Screen?

"My mother is trying to kill me," he said. "I need your help."

He heard his own mother's voice again, calling to him to wake up. Was it time for school? Had he slept too long. She would be so angry if he wasn't ready by the time she left for the hospital. Tom looked round, expecting to see his bedroom with its desk and bookshelf, but instead all he could see was the young man's face.

"You have to help me."

Charlie

There was no shelter that Charlie could crawl to. The building next to him was a blank concrete facade, darkened by pollution stains and interrupted only by air conditioners in upper storey windows. Parked cars lined the street, but any pedestrians must be hiding from the rain. There was no choice but to somehow get up onto his feet and walk. But every part of him hurt: his stomach, his ribs, his face, his arm, his kidneys. It wasn't the first beating he'd had and the memory of how long the blows would take to heal was not comforting. Knowing that Andrew Dwyer had something to hide wouldn't help him in the short term either.

The wall had no handholds to help pull himself up. There was nothing to do but to roll onto his hands and knees and push until he could get his legs underneath him. He did it at the price of a spinning head and another rush of blood in his mouth. He leaned against the concrete wall and waited for the nausea to pass.

Fuck, fuck, fuck, fuck.

Walking would keep him warmer, circulate his blood, and that would ease the worst of the pain. He hoped. So, he walked, step by stumbling step, with no idea where he was or where he was going. At least, he thought, the rain would wash the blood from his face, knees and hands. The Brutalist building beside him appeared to be an above-ground nuclear bunker with a mural of NYPD cops stuck to the side. Slowly it dawned on him that it must be a police station. Could he go in and ask for help? He thought about it. He remembered the police officers at the shooting and their lack of interest in his story, and the way the FBI had taken his clothes as if he were a suspect. Brody Murphy had faded into the background when he'd been kidnapped. There had been no police sirens following the delivery van. The thugs had pushed him out of the van here suggesting they were familiar with the area — did that mean they had friends in the police? Is that why Murphy had disappeared? Had he known? God, but he needed to think.

The sign at the cross street swam into view: 122nd. The flat was at 110th. He could walk twelve blocks — *anyone could walk twelve blocks* — and have a hot shower, put on some clean dry clothes and with luck there would be food.

The twelve blocks felt like the longest walk of his life. His clothes dragged against his sore skin, doubling in weight until he could barely lift his feet. As he walked, a few pedestrians appeared, hurrying with their umbrellas, taking no notice of him, ducking in and out of lighted shops. The scent of hot food made him salivate but he was too filthy to enter and he feared that if he once stopped moving, he would never re-start. Wales is known for rain. Rain made the hills green and the trees grow. Welsh rivers burst their banks every year. Charlie thought he knew rain. But this rain felt like a punishment for wearing the wrong clothes, for his lack of foresight, his assumption that the sunshine would last.

At last, he reached the apartment building, dimly aware of a police cruiser double parked on the opposite side of the street. The two shallow steps by the door almost defeated him, but he got to the front door and managed to extract the key from his sopping pocket with fingers frozen and unbending. By the time he got inside the flat, he was shaking with cold and fatigue. He collapsed onto the shoe bench by the door and began to peel off his wet things. Each garment resisted until he was sobbing with frustration, but he was finally naked, his wet things inside out on the floor by his feet.

And there they can stay.

Bruises were forming on his stomach and side. His knees and hands were scraped and reddened. His face just hurt, and he didn't plan to look in a mirror. A shower would help. If he could find the energy to walk the five or six steps to the bathroom and turn on the shower.

He managed it and the water was painful and wonderful at the same time. He could have stayed there for hours, except he couldn't.

The intercom buzzed. Charlie ignored it. It buzzed again. And again. And again.

In the end he gave in, dragging himself out into the hall and stepping over the tangled garments.

"What?" he snapped.

"Police. Open the door please."

No. Go away.

But he knew they wouldn't. He pressed the door release and went to his bedroom for a towel to wrap round his body. He kicked the wet clothes into the corner. When the buzzer rang on the flat door he was as ready as he could be.

Detective Marion Levine had brought a friend, another plain clothes woman who produced her badge wordlessly.

"Mr Rees," Levine said, "we'd like you to come with us to the police station to answer some questions."

Charlie had used the same words himself, many times.

They meant: "Don't make us arrest you, because we aren't quite ready for that yet, but you're coming with us whatever."

He sighed.

"Take a seat, ladies. I need to get dressed. You're welcome to watch if you think I'm going to run away. I think you can probably see I'm not armed."

The un-named officer blushed. And followed him along the wonky-floored corridor to the bedroom where she stood in the doorway and watched him dress, her hand resting on top of her gun.

TWENTY-ONE

TUESDAY 7.30PM

The police car took much less time to get back to the bunker of a police station than it had taken for Charlie to walk in the rain. Both Marion Levine and her un-named friend had been polite in escorting him to the car, though the un-named friend made sure he was aware of her weapon. He asked repeatedly why they wanted to talk to him and got no answers at all. Eventually, Levine shrugged and said, "The FBI are waiting for a warrant for your arrest. We're taking you in, but they have the questions." After that, nothing.

Inside, the building was brightly lit. It had to be; there was no natural light. Not on the ground floor anyway. Charlie probably shouldn't have been surprised that it felt familiar, even though the uniforms and accents were different, and more than half the officers were people of colour. And there were the guns. But it *felt* like a police station: scuffed floors, officers looking miserably at computer screens; the scent of burned coffee and the detritus from boxes of baked goods. He wondered if they were going to put him in a cell. They did, but they also offered coffee which he accepted, despite expecting it to be disgusting. Being dressed in dry clothes, and the padded jacket he'd hoped not to need, was better than being wet, but he was still cold. If the only hot drink on offer was horrible coffee, that's what he'd have. He wrapped himself in his jacket and thought about trying to find a lawyer. He still had his phone and wallet. They hadn't searched him, bar a walk through a metal detector, which made sense, given that they'd seen him get dressed.

Once Marion Levine had brought the coffee, he was alone. The cell could have been underground. It had no window and no sound filtered in from the outside. A bench ran along one side of the wall, with a thin mattress. There was a hole in the door with one way glass. If anyone was watching, all they would have seen was a fair-haired man with a bruised face huddled in a red padded coat. Charlie closed his eyes and tried to think.

Andrew Dwyer had warned Charlie off almost before Charlie had begun to investigate Kaylan's death. He knew who Dwyer was, but until a few hours ago, all he knew was that Dwyer was Kaylan's uncle, and that Sabrina credited him with helping her out financially. Now, he knew that Dwyer employed some extremely efficient thugs and he thought threatening Charlie with violence was a winning move. He also knew that Dwyer was involved in a construction project, though he didn't know exactly where. He could find that out. But the really interesting thing, Charlie thought, was how easily Dwyer's henchmen had found him in an obscure coffee shop close to the convention centre. Who had told them where he was? Evan from Sully Cybersecurity was one obvious candidate, though he'd seemed genuine. Presumably any of the other cybersecurity people could have followed them and alerted

Dwyer. Sabrina could have raised the alarm with her brother if she felt one of them was threatened. But Dwyer had warned Charlie about tarnishing Kaylan's reputation which was weird. Kaylan's reputation was already trashed and anyway he was dead. If the warning to Dwyer had come from Sabrina, the implication was that Dwyer or his cohorts had been following Charlie.

And of course, the other candidate for the role of betrayer-in-chief was Brody Murphy.

Murphy had disappeared into thin air. Admittedly Charlie had been distracted, but there had been no sign of Murphy from the moment the two heavies grabbed Charlie. Murphy was a cop. In this country he was armed, and in contact with other police officers. Wouldn't he have done *something*?

The coffee was as vile as Charlie had expected and by the time he drank it, it was lukewarm, coating his tongue with a taste of burnt metal, unpleasantly smooth. His hair had begun to dry damply against the collar of his coat. He felt his face gently; tapping his cheeks and the soft spots under his eyes. They hurt. If he could have brought himself to move, he could have looked at his reflection in the mirrored glass in the door to see how bad the damage was going to be. But he was still cold and his limbs were stiff, so he stayed where he was, huddling as deeply into his coat as he could and wishing for one of the big scarves he wore at home in winter. For all he knew, the cell might have been warm. He was cold to his bones.

The door rattled open, and a uniformed officer came in with what looked like an airline food tray, and more coffee. "Dinner," he said. Charlie said thanks and asked for a blanket. The officer disappeared and returned with a well boiled grey blanket and an even greyer pillow. Then Charlie was alone again with his thoughts. The coffee warmed his hands, and eventually his insides. The food he ignored. He wrapped himself in the blanket, and unexpectedly drifted into a fitful sleep. Much as on the previous day, Charlie lost all track of time.

The door opened so quietly that it took Charlie a moment to wake up. He scrabbled for his phone and saw it was almost six am.

"Come with me," Murphy said. "You need to get out of here before SA Mead turns up with his warrant."

Charlie turned his head. Murphy looked tired, though not as tired as Charlie felt.

"I'm serious. Let's go."

"You're a bit fucking late, Murphy. Who's going to be waiting outside this time?"

"I fucked up, okay? But if you're still here when Mead arrives, things will get much worse. I'm what you've got."

The only one of the whole boiling that Charlie trusted was Marion Levine. When she said the FBI was coming with a warrant for his arrest, he believed her. He slowly pushed himself to his feet. His stomach muscles screamed and his feet throbbed.

"I don't know what your game is. It's time for an explanation."

"Outside, and I'll tell you. Quick."

Charlie heard voices through the open door. He didn't know who they were but the possibility they might be coming for him made him move. One night in a police cell was one night too many. Murphy grabbed his arm and pulled him through the door, letting it swing closed behind them. He hustled Charlie along the corridor and through an airlock to a fenced-in car park. Murphy's small saloon was parked right by the door.

"Get in the back and get down on the floor," Murphy ordered.

There were shouts from inside the bunker.

Did he have a choice?

"You can sit up now," Murphy said.

Charlie wasn't sure he could. He had wedged himself in the footwell behind the front seats. The carpet smelt of dust and disinfectant and, if possible, the seats smelled worse. The space under the passenger seat was filled with crumpled fast-food wrappers, some of which had been there long enough to breed new life forms. To get into the space, he'd had to crunch his sore and bruised stomach and he suspected that un-crunching it was going to hurt even more. He could sense his hair lying in all that filth and it made his skin crawl. It shouldn't have mattered that he was wearing one of his last sets of clean clothes, but it did. If he'd been convinced of the necessity for any of this, he could have ignored all the dirt and discomfort. But things were becoming more surreal by the minute. He struggled onto his hands and knees, resenting the foul carpet under his scraped hands. By wrapping his arms around the passenger seat, he dragged himself upward. Out of the window, he saw the familiar entrance to his apartment building.

"Is this *Groundhog Day?*" Charlie asked. "I go into the flat in the hope of a shower and a coffee and some bastard turns up to arrest me?"

Murphy turned round to look at Charlie. "You'll be safe for an hour or two at least. Long enough for a shower."

"Long enough for you to tell me what's going on?"

In answer, Murphy got out of the car, and held the door open for Charlie. "I'm assuming you've still got the key?"

He had, and he let them into the building. They stood silently as the lift wheezed its way to the top floor. Once in the flat, Murphy said he'd make coffee while Charlie showered.

"Look for food and painkillers," Charlie instructed. Murphy nodded.

CHARLIE GOT himself clean at the price of too much pain. His knees were almost too stiff to climb into the tub, and the hot water on his scrapes and bruises was almost too much to bear. A shave was out of the question. He didn't even want to look at his face let alone scrape a razor over it. Cleaning his teeth was a delicate operation, but he managed not to re-open the tear on the inside of his cheek. He patted himself dry enough to get dressed before following the smell of coffee to the living room. Murphy was pacing from end to end of the room. Their coffee, plus a plate of cold pizza slices and a bag of doughnuts sat on one of the side tables. Tom's jacket and messenger bag lay on the sofa. Charlie put them both on his lap, taking comfort from the smell of Old Spice and pencil shavings.

"Now. I need to know what's going on. Like who you are for a start." Charlie helped himself to food and took a slurp of his coffee.

"It's ... complicated," Murphy said. "But I'm on your side. That's as much as I can say."

"You weren't on my side when Dwyer and his cohorts were kidnapping me," Charlie said. "And I have to wonder how they knew where to find me. Sorry, mate, but *it's complicated* doesn't cut it."

Murphy put his coffee down. "I didn't tell them where to find you. I was as surprised as you."

"Why am I having trouble believing that? No one else knew where we were going."

"All I can do is ask you to trust me. I got you out of the police station before Special Agent Mead turned up with his warrant, and believe me, you do not want to be arrested for suspected murder. Because that's what the warrant says."

Charlie leapt to his feet and immediately felt as if he'd taken another blow to the stomach. His head swam and he fell back into the chair.

"Who the fuck am I supposed to have murdered?"

By contrast, Murphy was calm. "Kaylan Sully. No one thinks you actually murdered him, but better not to be arrested for it."

"There are a dozen witnesses to say I didn't murder anyone. Two people thanked me for saving them after Kaylan was killed right before their eyes."

"But that's not the evidence the FBI are relying on. They are relying on the fact that they found a gun in this apartment." Murphy held up his hand to forestall another explosion from Charlie. "Of course, you didn't have a gun. But a gun was found here. That doesn't make it yours. It could equally belong to Orianna. Or Tom. And there's nothing to connect this gun to the bookstore — yet. But it's enough for the warrant, and if you're arrested you won't be getting bail because anyone can see you're a flight risk." Murphy shrugged. "So, better not be anywhere you can be arrested."

"Like here," Charlie said flatly. He wasn't sure he believed

Murphy, or that he trusted him, but was it a risk he was willing to take? Probably not.

"Like here, or the hospital where Tom is. I think they're serious, so I'd suggest not using your cell phone either."

"They'd track my *phone?*"

"Not only could they track your phone, they could involve the US Marshals."

Charlie had only the sketchiest idea of who the US Marshals were but what he did know was that they had almost unlimited powers. He felt sick. He'd been in the city for just over a week. Tom was in a coma in hospital, and he, Charlie, was wanted for a crime he patently hadn't committed. The only way he could get the FBI off his back for good was to find who had killed Kaylan and the other man. And he couldn't do that with the FBI tracking his every move, not to mention Andrew Dwyer and his minions... who seemed to know how to find him more easily even than law enforcement.

"I'm fucked."

"Pretty much," Murphy said, walking over to the window and looking out. "Actually, you're totally fucked. The Feds are getting out of their cars downstairs."

It looked like Murphy had set Charlie up once more. *Here we go again.* He kicked Murphy in the balls, snatched up his coat, Tom's things and ran.

Downstairs was not an option. There was a back door to the apartments, but the only way to get to it was through the lobby. Charlie headed upstairs to the roof. He and Tom been up here once, just for a look. There were a few pots of flowers and a couple of deck chairs next to a sign saying the roof was out of bounds. The top of the lift shaft was there, as well as other odd protuberances whose purposes Charlie guessed were to do with heating and water. The buildings in this area weren't skyscrapers and Charlie felt the sky all around him. Much too much sky. Noises from the streets below travelled upward, but he had no desire to go and look over the edge. As he'd learned last year, clambering about on high buildings was not his super-power. At least the rain had stopped. Maybe he could just hide. Because everything fucking hurt.

Nice idea. Except if I can see the marble staircase leading upward, so can the FBI.

Maybe hiding would give him the chance to sneak past them while they were busy in his flat. Maybe. His heart was beating overtime in his chest and he could feel the sweat break out under his arms.

The one thing he could do was block the door. He was about to wedge one of the deckchairs under the door handle and trying to control the whimpers that threatened to give away his whereabouts. But someone was pushing against the door from the other side.

"Open the fucking door," Murphy growled. "I'm on your side."

Charlie fell back. If Murphy yelled, he could bring the FBI onto the roof in seconds. He wanted to trust Murphy, but not without getting some answers. The door opened and Charlie grabbed Murphy by the collar, pulling him onto the roof and shoving the door closed behind them.

"You kicked me, asshole," Murphy said when he'd helped Charlie bar the door. Charlie could see him wince when they bent over to wedge the deck chair more securely.

"You abandoned me to Dwyer's thugs. You know who I am, but all I ever get from you is lies. You pretend to help, then you dob me in. I don't believe you're NYPD."

"No. I'm not. But I am law enforcement. And I'm under-cover, so let's get out of here before the FBI work out where you've gone."

"This is the last time, Murphy." Murphy seemed to get the sub-text. *Betray me again and I'll do more than kick you in the nuts.*

Patsy would climb down the side of the building, he thought, and shuddered. But the building next door did look as if it was connected to this one. He put his coat on and squashed Tom's jacket into the messenger bag. It wasn't going to be easy to carry, but he wasn't leaving it. Charlie didn't want to run across the roof in case he was directly above the flat and his steps told the FBI exactly where they were. And he'd used up all his running energy getting this far. So, he walked as quietly as he could to where the building next door was — thank all the gods — joined to his. Murphy followed, silently. Charlie felt obscurely better for having him there, but then he had felt better the last time too.

To get on to the next building, they had to climb over a parapet. The building was the length of several football pitches. One more roof the size of this one, and they would be at the end of the street and might escape. Now they could run, and did, despite their injuries. At the end Charlie saw the next building *was* connected, but after that there was a gap for the cross street. This time the neighbouring roof was at least six feet lower. Only the thought of being imprisoned for God knows how long while trying to prove his innocence made him climb over the parapet and let go. He fell ungracefully, scraping his already sore hands on the wall. But he was down. Murphy followed, landing less awkwardly, but still a long way from the surefooted Patsy. Charlie had a spike of longing for his team, even Eddy, the big lump. He smiled at the thought of Eddy galloping along and complaining all the way.

"What are you grinning at?" Murphy asked.

"I was thinking about a colleague. Someone I trust." *Unlike you.*

Murphy didn't say anything else.

Now he had to find some stairs into the building, and hope he'd come far enough. This running across the rooftops was best kept for movies.

This roof was clearly in constant use. There were clothes lines, a picnic table and chairs, as well lots of pots with green shoots popping out of the soil. There was a door, and it was open, and it led to a set of stairs winding round the lift shaft.

There was also a blue New York Yankees baseball cap hanging on the door. Charlie stowed it under his jacket. He ran down the stairs, holding the banister rail as his knees protested. At each of the landings he paused to listen, but there was no one around. Unlike in his own building, these stairs went all the way down to the yard where the bins were kept and Charlie went all the way down with them. He heard Murphy's steps padding down behind him. If they went out and the door closed behind them, there would be no way back. He had to trust that the bin yard would have a way out to the street away from the eyes of his pursuers.

Luck was on his side. He put the blue cap on, pulling the brim low, risking a quick glance back down the street to his apartment building. There was no sign of any activity, thought there were a couple more black cars than usual double-parked. Time to get some coffee and regroup.

Coffee was the easy part, along with a toasted bagel from a street vendor. He wasn't letting Murphy out of his sight, so Charlie found a bench on the west side of Central Park for eating and regrouping purposes. It was chilly, though the rain was holding off. Everything ached where he'd been hit, and his face was clearly a disaster zone given the way the vendor had looked at him. Some large sunglasses would probably help with that. He needed access to a phone the FBI didn't know about, enough cash to get through the next few days and somewhere safe to stay off the radar. If he couldn't prove his innocence in that time ... He *would* prove his innocence.

The first requirement was cash and a phone. Then he was going to retrace his steps, starting with Sabrina Sully, and then, one way or another, he was going to find out who Brody Murphy really was. His instincts told him that Murphy was one of the good guys, and that he was telling the truth when he claimed to be law enforcement. At the same time, reason said

Murphy had told Dwyer where to find Charlie, and possibly told the FBI the same thing. Could he *really* believe anything Murphy said? That there was a warrant for his arrest had been confirmed by Marion Levine, but the nature of the warrant? That was all Murphy. Murphy was going to have to talk.

TWENTY-FOUR

WEDNESDAY 10AM

Tom

It was as if he was looking up through the water to the daylight above the surface. Sunlight danced on the top of the water, though down here it was blue and dark. Tom heard people calling him to swim upward to the light. He thought about it. It was very comfortable down here in the depths. A voice said, "You were shot," and he remembered. Charlie shouting. Remembered pushing Orianna to the floor, trying to keep her safe. Shots sounding like a heavy-duty staple gun. The smell of spilled drinks. Whimpering. Then pain like he'd never felt before and the sound of Orianna shouting for Charlie. *I must have passed out from the pain.* He couldn't remember what happened next.

"I was shot," he said. Charlie had been shot once and had carried on as if nothing had happened, but he wasn't Charlie. "I was shot," he said again. All at once the voices from the surface became a clamour, begging him to swim, swim up to the light.

He tried to listen, to separate out the voices. One of them sounded like his mother, but that couldn't be right. None of them sounded like Charlie. A thought floated into his head. *I'm in New York with Charlie.* His mother couldn't be there and the voices and the light were an illusion. No way was he going to leave the embrace of soft blue darkness for an illusion.

But somewhere inside, he knew it wasn't an illusion, and that he could choose to start swimming if he wanted to. Did he want to? He wanted to see Charlie. Only Charlie wasn't there.

Charlie

The spot Charlie chose in Central Park was close to where he and Tom had sat on the day of the shooting. Tom had been rocking his lumberjack look — red plaid shirt, baggy jeans and battered leather hiking boots. Shirtsleeves rolled up to show off his ink. Charlie had dozed while Tom sketched and then without having to talk about it, they had gone back to the flat, cool after the hot sun outside, and gone to bed. Charlie had unbuttoned the red shirt and run his hands over Tom's chest, hardly able to swallow from desire, pinching Tom's nipples because he knew Tom liked it, loving the hair under his fingers, and in turn loving Tom's hands on his own, smoother skin, making him shiver. Tom tangled his hands in Charlie's hair, using it to pull Charlie closer. They lay together, touching along the length of their bodies, caressing and exploring, reconnecting, kissing slowly and breaking off to smile and then kiss some more. Tom said he wanted to be fucked, so that's what they did. Charlie remembers how it felt, watching Tom gasp as he felt Charlie inside him, moving from slow and sensuous to hot and sweaty and *urgent*, Tom yelling his name and all the world narrowed into a single point, the point of contact between their bodies where nothing else mattered. Charlie's orgasm had crashed over him like an avalanche of feeling. He didn't know where he ended, and Tom began. His senses were full of Tom: the feel of his skin, the smell of his skin, the taste of his skin, the sound of his voice, and the look in his eyes as he came undone.

Charlie had moved into Tom's bed, then into his house and his life without ever considering what it meant except that Tom knew what he wanted, and Charlie loved him. He'd never gone beyond that. Now Tom was lying in hospital, and Charlie was on the run. What had seemed simple at home — being together — wasn't a given any more.

I have to put this first, because if I don't, I lose everything.

It was as if he had rubbed the sleep out of his eyes could see himself and Tom clearly for the first time, and realised it had all become much more important than he had ever suspected.

"EARTH TO CHARLIE REES." Charlie started out of his daydream at Murphy's words.

"I was thinking," Charlie said.

"From your expression, not about the case."

"About my partner, Tom. We're supposed to be on holiday."

"Not what you had in mind for the trip, I'm guessing." Pause. "Does Tom own that apartment?"

Yep, he could be a copper. Always with the questions.

Charlie smiled. "I wish. An art foundation owns it, and people like Tom get to use it as a place to work in New York."

"He's an artist, then, your Tom?"

"Printmaker. Well known at home. But he's also the principal of an art college. Which I bet you already knew."

Murphy had the grace to blush. His pale skin lit up like

neon and Charlie was reminded of Patsy's preference for loud pink clothes when not in uniform.

"I knew he was in charge of an art school, but not the other stuff."

"You'd have found out, though. You're invested in me and in something about this case, but it isn't Kaylan's murder because you don't believe he was the target. The way you disappeared when Dwyer's thugs turned up makes me think that perhaps it's Dwyer you're interested in. Am I right?"

Murphy looked away, apparently fascinated by a couple walking an undulating sea of small, curly-haired dogs.

"Dwyer may be of interest to law enforcement," was all he said. But it was more than he'd said in the past. "I have to go, but I've got something for you." He reached into the inside pocket of his jacket. The something turned out to be a new smartphone, still in its packaging, and a well-used phone-sized power bank, lights indicating that it was fully charged. Charlie took them both.

"So, now you can track me?"

"So, now I can call you, and you can call me. Charlie, I swear to you, I'm on your side." He took a pen from his pocket and scribbled a number on the package. "My number. I have to go and rescue the car. Stay safe." And with that, Murphy stood up and walked out of the park.

Probably to tell someone where I am. But fuck it, let me sit still for five minutes.

IF HE COULD KEEP out of the way of the FBI, he stood some chance of finding out who had killed Kaylan and why. Andrew Dwyer had to be at the top of his list, with some unknown person at Sully Cybersecurity running a close second. Before any of that, he wanted to find out who Brody Murphy was, or wasn't. He unwrapped the phone, inserted the SIM card and plugged it in to the power bank. Then he called a familiar number, hoping that Patsy would answer. She did, in a voice that indicated she expected to be told about picking up a parcel she hadn't ordered.

"I heard about Tom, and the shooting," she said when she realised who it was. "Are you okay?"

"Not really. I will tell you about it, I promise, but is Unwin around?" Charlie asked.

"What can I do for you?" Unwin asked when Patsy handed the phone over. Charlie thought he heard the rustle of bed covers.

"Can you find out if someone is a police officer? His name is Brody Murphy, and that's all I know. He has an NYPD shield, and he appears to have access to their information systems, but there's something not right. I think he's one of the good guys, but I need to be sure."

"On it," Unwin said, as if nothing were simpler. "Anything else?"

Charlie thought. He could find out more about Andrew Dwyer himself, but Unwin would be faster, and any trail he left wouldn't lead straight back to Charlie's location. Though he doubted Unwin would leave a trail. "A guy called Andrew Dwyer," he said. "Kaylan Sully's uncle and almost certainly some kind of crook."

"Ring you back on this number?" Unwin asked, and when Charlie said yes, the call ended.

Thirty seconds later, the new phone rang, and he heard Unwin's voice.

"That Brody Murphy? That'll be Special Agent Murphy to you."

Charlie stared at the phone in his hand and had to make an effort not to allow his jaw to drop open.

Does not compute.

"But that's all I can get," Unwin continued. "I can't find out which bit of the FBI he works for, yet, but the phone number is to the switchboard at Quantico. Your guess is as good as mine."

Charlie stayed where he was when Unwin ended the call. He was in so far over his head that he couldn't imagine the surface, let alone see it. Talking to Unwin, hearing Patsy's voice made him long for the familiarity of home, people he knew and trusted, and places he could go to be safe. Places to be safe probably didn't include this particular spot, he thought. Time to get moving, though he had no idea where. He picked up Tom's bag, then decided to get himself organised before he left. First thing was to remove the SIM card from his own phone and put Murphy's number in the new one. Then he re-folded Tom's jacket to make it all less bulky. Tom's phone he left at the bottom of the bag, but his wallet went into Charlie's pocket. It was thick with cash, and if push came to shove, Charlie would have no qualms about using Tom's cards. He considered going to the hospital and arguing his way in on the basis of being Tom's emergency contact. How bad could Verity Pennant be? It wasn't like he didn't have experience of dealing with disapproving mothers. Except the police were probably waiting for him at the hospital. He let his head fall backward and closed his eyes with a groan. The words to a song wafted into his head. Something about being a legal alien in New York. Only he wasn't sure he was legal any more.

THE PHONE VIBRATED against his thigh for several seconds before Charlie registered what it was. By the time he had it out of his pocket, the call had gone to voicemail. It was Brody Murphy, and Charlie called him back.

"Hey, Charlie. I've had a call. There's something we ought to see."

"What? Another way you can set me up?" Charlie asked, but his heart wasn't in it. If the only company on offer was Murphy, he'd take it, at least for now.

"Some colleagues may have located the person who sent those emails to Orianna. I'll come and pick you up."

The drive took about twenty minutes. Murphy parked beside a high chain link fence bisected by a gate with a magnetic lock. Behind the fence was a tall, un-ornamented, brick slab of a building, with windows set with appalling regularity into the blank walls. It could have been anything. Offices, a prison, a police station, Russian housing from the Soviet Era. Charlie judged it against the exuberant decoration of most New York buildings and found it wanting.

"How do we get in there?" he asked Murphy.

"With one of these. We're going to see a Ms Deganway, who lives with her son Hannibal. These are apartments for low-income residents."

Murphy produced an electronic fob.

The flat they were visiting was on the ground floor with windows concealed by a combination of thick metal bars and

air conditioning units. Through the open front door, the inside
was dark. Murphy called out a greeting:

"NYPD, Ms Deganway, may we come in?"

The rooms Charlie could see appeared generous: a living
room with doors leading from it to two bedrooms, bathroom
and what looked to be another bizarrely small kitchen. Everything was neat and clean as far as he could tell in the gloom.

A woman, presumably Hannibal's mother, sat on a plastic
covered sofa in the living room. She looked to Charlie as if she
had dark skin, but the room itself was so dark it was difficult to
tell. She could have been made from stone for all the notice she
took of their entrance.

"Hello, Mrs Deganway," Charlie said.

"It's Miss," she replied. "Get on with it and get out." Her
voice was flat and without inflection or anger.

"Thank you," Charlie said, embarrassed. He followed
Murphy as he opened one of the doors. Charlie saw a neatly
made single bed, with a white sheet folded over a blue blanket
and a white covered pillow. A dining chair was tucked under a
small table on which sat piles of magazines and newspapers.
Double doors indicated a closet. And then there were the walls.
They were covered from floor to ceiling with pictures of
women. Not naked women, or women in provocative poses.
Mostly faces, though some full body shots. Some were publicity
stills on glossy photographic paper, others cut from magazines
or newspapers, and others printed on plain paper. About half
the pictures were of Orianna. Charlie didn't recognise the other
women, though he did note that all of them shared Orianna's
directness of expression.

"Let me guess, a gallery of women poets?" Charlie asked.

"Lesbian, bisexual, trans and self-identified queer women
poets," Murphy replied. He indicated the table. "With lists of

where they are all scheduled to read, or do book signings. Including Orianna on Sunday night."

"It doesn't prove anything," Charlie said. "Except an interest in poetry."

"He's coming up on forty, living at home with his mother, does a dead-end job ... classic."

"All potatoes are vegetables. All vegetables are not potatoes."

"What?" Murphy squeaked.

"Just because every serial killer and nutcase with a gun has an obsession with his victims, doesn't mean that everyone obsessed with, say, lesbian poets is a killer. Does he have a gun? Does he have an alibi? Does he even have a computer? Because I don't see one."

Charlie moved up to one of the walls and looked at it closely. "Look here," he said, pointing. He took Murphy's arm to show him the wall. "When do you think these pictures were put up?"

"I dunno," Murphy said.

"Don't you think if they'd been put up more than a few hours ago that some of the corners might be lifting? Or that they might be getting discoloured? These pictures were all put up at the same time, and not very long ago. God, Brody, the glue is still damp. Have you talked to this man's mother about it? What does she have to say?"

"Come on, Charlie, this is straight out of the textbooks."

Isn't it just? Charlie thought. Who has been reading the textbooks? Brody Murphy, or someone else?

TWENTY-SIX
WEDNESDAY NOON

A detailed search of Hannibal's room produced no evidence of a gun, computer or car ownership. His mother insisted that her son couldn't drive, and had neither gun nor computer. As for the wall art, she simply shrugged, and could not be drawn on when or why the decoration had been done. It was his own business what Hannibal did in his room, she said, with a face as unmoving as stone. She showed no visible sign of being worried about her son, or even particularly resentful at the invasion of her privacy by two police officers. She didn't like it, but there were none of the protests Charlie was used to. She hadn't even watched them search. She made no objection when Murphy put police tape across the door to the bedroom.

"Where is Hannibal now?" Charlie asked.

Another shrug.

"Out. At work, probably. Or with a friend. He's a grown man. You want him, you find him."

Charlie could see Murphy struggling with his temper.

"Thanks, Miss Deganway," he said, and with a hand to Murphy's elbow, led him towards the door.

"She knows when he did those walls," Murphy growled.

"Perhaps. But she's not going to tell us. Not without a better reason than *we want to know*. The person we should ask is Hannibal, and that means we have to find him." Not that Charlie expected to be able to find Hannibal. Mainly because he wasn't convinced that Hannibal existed.

"He works not far from here. Shelf-stacking."

There was a chirp as Murphy unlocked his car doors. The car was black, of a make Charlie didn't recognise. The interior showed all the signs of a person who spent too long sitting in the driver's seat: an insulated travel cup by the gearstick, crumpled takeaway wrappers on the passenger seat, and a charging cable hanging from the dashboard. The overwhelming smell was of air freshener from a tree-shaped tag hanging from the rear-view mirror. Charlie thought of the times his own car had been like this. He moved the rubbish to the footwell and got in, glad he was in a seat and not back on the floor.

"Wait," he said when Murphy began to fasten his seatbelt. "How did you come to be at Hannibal's flat? Who told you to look there?"

Murphy blushed red. "Tip-off. Anonymous."

"You're not finding all this a bit convenient? Suspiciously convenient?"

"It hardly matters how we got the information if it's good information," Murphy said.

"How much do you want to bet we don't find Hannibal at his workplace? Because this stinks, Brody. The glue was hardly dry on those pictures, and you said it yourself, *textbook*. The question is, who's trying to fool who here? You need to get your story straight. Either you tracked Hannibal down from his email address, or you got a tip-off."

CHARLIE WANTED to believe Murphy was honest, but the evidence wasn't on Murphy's side. Again. He berated himself for falling for another of Murphy's set-ups. "I can see that it might look bad," Murphy said.

"You think?"

"There's a turf war going on between the FBI and NYPD. We're supposed to work together, but it's not easy. I just go where I'm sent."

"So, who sent you to look at this set-up? And who told you to bring me along?"

Murphy looked away, out of the window and back towards the apartment building. "I don't know who got the tip-off, but I got sent because our precinct is the closest to here and to the bookstore. It was my idea to contact you. I thought ... I thought it was genuine."

"If you'd thought that, you'd have called the circus, not me," Charlie said.

"The circus?"

"Forensics, your FBI contacts, your bosses, I don't know. You'd have searched the rest of the flat. You're fucking with me Brody, either willingly or because you're being made to do it. We're done here." Charlie opened the car door to get out.

This time it was Murphy who called, "Wait. Look, I honestly don't know what's going on," he said with a tone of desperation in his voice. "I thought the precinct *would* send the circus as you call it. I'm sure they will come. I just thought you'd want to see it before they all arrived."

"But you're not going to wait for them?"

"I thought finding Deganway was more important."

"If you say so," Charlie said and exited the car, slamming the door closed behind him. He still couldn't decide whether Murphy was an active participant in this farce but either way Charlie wanted to get to the hospital to check on Tom. He also felt the need to talk to someone he *did* trust in the hope of finding his way through the tangle of stories. Ignoring Murphy in the car following him, Charlie began to walk in what he hoped was the direction of the hospital. If a cab came along, he'd hail it, otherwise he'd just walk. He didn't recognise any of the street names or numbers, but the grid system told him he was going the right way. There were apparently no taxis in this part of the city, or not at this time of day anyway. He settled into a rhythm, as the streetscape changed from the blank, brick-built facades secured behind chain link, to more familiar tenement blocks, albeit less prosperous than the area around their flat and the hospital. The streets weren't busy. A few people were walking dogs, or carrying shopping, and there were the ubiquitous oddballs in ill-fitting clothes and broken shoes, or pushing a shopping trolley full of rubbish, or muttering to themselves. The sounds of sirens drifted toward him, along with bursts of music from passing vehicles.

A homeless man was sitting on a step with his possessions around him and a cardboard sign asking for money. Charlie felt for the five-dollar bill he kept in his pocket for just this occasion, pulled it out and leaned over to give it to the man. He saw the man's eyes widen and his mouth open at the same time as he heard the shot.

For the second time in less than a week, Charlie dived for cover, pushing the homeless man down in front of him. He heard the crack of another shot, and then another. The homeless man pulled at him, half dragging him behind the steps he'd been sitting on. There was another shot. Something sharp hit his cheek and he felt blood under his fingers when he touched it. The next thing they heard were sirens in the distance and a car accelerating away,

"Motherfucker. Some fucker's trying to kill me."

On past evidence, more likely they were trying to kill me.

The homeless man didn't smell great, but Charlie wasn't going to let go of him until he was sure the shooters had gone. There were a few yells from behind them.

"Get off me," the man said.

Charlie did, mostly so he could look round at whoever was shouting. If someone planned to shoot him, he wanted to at least see them. But none of the gathering crowd were waving guns.

"What happened?" People were asking. "Did you see?" A

woman pulled two school-age children away from the crowd, and berated them for their curiosity.

The homeless man sat back on his step, and it was Charlie's turn to ask what happened.

"Some motherfuckers in a fancy car, that's what happened. Poking a fucking gun out of the window. Motherfuckers."

"Shooting the homeless," came a voice from the crowd, and several others joined in agreement.

"Has anyone called the police?" Charlie asked.

No one answered. Charlie got his new phone out and pressed 911. As he waited for the reply, he saw the watchers begin to disperse. The homeless man started gathering his possessions. Charlie cut off the call.

"What's going on?" he asked. "Someone just tried to shoot us."

"And they've fucking gone. No way am I waiting round for another set of fucking murderers to show up. Some mother-fucker tries to kill me, but I'll be the one with five cops on my back."

Charlie looked around. His was the only white face. He put the phone back in his pocket.

"No police, then," he said.

The man breathed out and sat back down on his step.

"Did you see the make of the car?" Charlie asked.

"Black SUV with some chrome on the side. Pimp car," came the answer.

"Did you see who was shooting?"

"I was too busy being knocked off my feet. I should sue you for pushing me down."

"Do it," Charlie said with a grin. "I'll explain to the judge how I was saving your life." He got a half-smile in return. "Then you saved mine, dragging me behind those steps." He held out his hand. "Thank you."

"They weren't trying to shoot Miro." Charlie turned round to see that one of the bystanders, a Black man in a tracksuit with dreadlocks showing beneath a wooly hat, had moved closer.

"What makes you say that?" Charlie asked.

"Because it's true, stranger. That guy coulda shot Miro the first two times he drove by. He was waiting for you."

Charlie's blood ran cold.

"You got lucky my friend. Still, you can go away now. We've got enough trouble of our own." The man wasn't hostile, but he wasn't friendly either. Charlie thought he had exhausted his chances of getting more questions answered. But he asked one anyway.

"Did you see the shooter?"

The man shook his head. His expression was beginning to harden.

"I was hoping for a taxi," Charlie said.

The man jerked his head. "Next block. Ya might get a cab. There's a bus going downtown." The man stood with his feet planted firmly on the pavement and his hands on his hips. Charlie had worn out any welcome he might have had.

"Thanks," Charlie said, and began to walk, feeling eyes on his back as he went.

Someone in a black SUV with chrome on the side had tried to shoot him, or at least tried to frighten him. The bookshop shooter had driven off in a black SUV with chrome on the sides. Charlie didn't believe in coincidences, not like this one, anyway. Murphy had known where Charlie was, but it wasn't Murphy who had shot at him. Had Murphy told the shooter where to find him, or had the shooter already known?

At the end of the block, he reached a north-south avenue, with all the traffic heading south. The rain started again, without warning. Clear sky to bouncing off the pavements in the blink of an eye. A bus drew in to the side of the street and people began to get on and off. Charlie joined them. He tapped one of Tom's cards on the reader and found a seat by the window. Outside, the rain streaked the window with diagonal dashes until it was obscured as if by a net curtain. Charlie stared out, unable to make out much through the murk, with no real idea about where he was going. A mechanical voice reeled off the street numbers, winding down as they progressed towards midtown. The rain got heavier.

The mechanical voice had now reached numbers Charlie recognised. They were close to the Empire State Building.

This part of the city was crowded, a steady stream of people entering and leaving, closing and opening their umbrellas as they got on and off the bus. Charlie caught sight of himself in the window. He had a smear of dried blood on his cheek and his hair was dark and flattened by the rain. His trousers clung to his thighs where the rain had soaked through and though his jacket had done remarkably well, his shirt was wet around his neck. At least his feet were still dry. He could stay on the bus where it was safe, and no one knew where he was. At least until the rain stopped. Then he could decide what to do.

The bus continued south, past midtown and the lights and bustle of shops, until Charlie had no idea where he was. What he wanted to do was to go to the hospital and force his way into Tom's room. And he would do it, just not until later. But first he needed to look at that flat again. Something was wrong about it, and he didn't just mean the fake serial-killer-wall-of-obsession. He got off the bus into the rain, walked until he found the northbound bus stop and climbed aboard the first bus that came. The street numbers began to increase as the bus wound its way north. At 115th he got off. There were several of the blank-looking apartment buildings nearby, so he knew he was in the right area. He just had to find the one with the Deganways' apartment. It took him half an hour, and then he was on the wrong side of the chain link fence with no way of getting in.

Eventually someone came out, and Charlie was through the gate. The rain was his friend. No one wanted to hang around to ask him his business, though the small group of teenagers did give him an odd look. Charlie suspected that most of the white people in this area were cops, and let's face it, he was probably giving off all the cop vibes. He wasn't quite in Eddie's spot-the-cop league, but no one was ever surprised when he said what he did for a living.

The next obstacle was the main door to the apartment building, only for a miracle it was open. Propped open by a fire extinguisher. Charlie blessed whoever it was who had lost their keys, or who had nipped out with the rubbish or whatever. He was in. The internal corridor was dark. Sounds of TVs and music seeped from the individual front doors, along with the smell of weed and cigarette smoke. The Deganways' apartment was past the bank of lifts and Charlie met no one as he made his way there. He could hear one of the lifts approaching as he lifted his hand to knock on the door. There was no obvious reason for Charlie to hide from whoever was in the lift, but some instinct made him duck into the deepest shadow. Probably a response to having been shot at in the street. He heard the lift doors opening and footsteps going to the main doorway. A man's voice cursed the rain, and Charlie was alone again, staring at the door—which wasn't properly closed. He must have noticed subconsciously. Of course, there could be an innocent explanation, but the way the hairs were standing up on the back of his neck told Charlie that there wasn't.

Still, he knocked. No answer.

"Miss Deganway," he called. No answer. "It's Charlie Rees, I was here earlier," he called, and then he pushed the door open.

THE AIR in the room was still. Charlie didn't move. He let himself take in the scene. Miss Deganway wasn't there, and there was no sign of anyone else. In fact, there was no sign that anyone had ever been there at all. The plastic-covered sofa showed no indentations. No dust marred any of the flat surfaces. There were no fingermarks on the black glass of the TV. The tiny kitchen was clear of glasses or coffee cups, and what he should have noticed on his first visit — there was no hum from the huge refrigerator. He had thought Hannibal's room was a stage set and he'd been right. The whole place was a stage set and Miss Deganway had been an actor.

CHARLIE HEARD SIRENS FROM OUTSIDE. It wasn't an unusual sound, but he had a powerful urge to run. If the police were coming here, Charlie wanted to be somewhere else.

The sirens got closer.

Charlie snatched up Tom's messenger bag. The teenagers had seen him come off the street, but no one had seen him enter the flat. Yes, he was a police officer, albeit a Welsh one, but this felt all kinds of wrong. This whole day felt wrong, like someone was pulling the strings off-stage, and only they knew what happened in the rest of the puppet show.

Reason told him that he could prove his innocence of Kaylan's murder. But it would all take time, and Charlie had a sense that time was running out, that events were accelerating. He needed to think and to try to make sense of what he'd found out over the last few days. Above all, he needed to know what was going on at the hospital and to know that Tom was safe.

It was too late. The sirens stopped. He could hear people shouting and see the reflections of blue lights on the walls of the dark corridor. Any moment the police would be in the building.

A green light showed one of the lifts was on the ground floor. Charlie pressed the button and when the doors opened, he got in and hit the button for the top floor. The doors closed as the first uniformed officers came through the main entrance, guns drawn.

Charlie's legs went from under him and he sank onto the floor of the lift, head spinning. What the fuck was he supposed to do now?

CHARLIE SAT on the fire exit stairs at the top of the apartment building. The concrete was chilly, but his jacket was warm, if damp, and the stairs themselves were clean. When he got out of the lift, he could hear voices from within the flats, the voices of people getting on with ordinary lives. The voice he most wanted to hear was Tom's but at that moment he was lonely enough to talk to his mother. Not that he would. It was late in the UK, and five minutes listening to his mother describe Charlie's faults would be enough to drive him to complete despair. Instead, he dialed a familiar number.

"Sir, it's Charlie."

God only knew what time it was in the UK, but Kent must be at home and had probably been asleep.

"Is everything alright?"

"Yes, but ... not really." Where was he supposed to start? Mal Kent had warned him off once already, told him not to interfere. "Sorry, sir. It's too late to ring. It's not important." He ended the call and put the phone back in his pocket, and wondered how long he would have to sit where he was before trying to get out of the building.

His phone rang.

"Charlie. You're not ringing me because you like the sound of my voice. Is Tom okay?" Kent sounded worried, and Charlie wanted to cry.

"I don't know. They won't let me see him. They won't tell me anything. His parents, I mean."

"But he's ...?"

"Alive. Yes. But he's in a coma."

"Charlie, don't give up. That's an order. Now tell me why you rang." Charlie heard music in the background, imagined Mal at home with his fiancé, cuddled up on the sofa, as he would have been with Tom. He felt the tears behind his eyes and blinked hard. A door closed on the other side of the world, and the music stopped. A chair scraped against a hard floor. "Charlie. What do you need? Bail money? A character reference? A lawyer? Who do I need to call?"

Charlie took a deep breath and tried to get his thoughts in order.

"I need to find out who someone is. His name is Brody Murphy, and he says he's with the NYPD, only he isn't. I've asked Unwin already; all he can find is that he's really FBI. I don't know if he's trying to help me or get me killed." Charlie recounted the day's events: the visit to Hannibal Deganway's apartment, the apparently 'perfect' serial killer set-up, the drive-by shooting. "I know you told me not to get involved, but I *am* involved. The FBI took my clothes. Murphy says they found a gun in my flat. They seem to think I killed Kaylan. Or maybe they just want me to think that. I don't know."

"It doesn't sound like you know much. It *does* sound like someone wants you out of the way. I'll see what I can find out, though no promises. Go and see Tom."

If they'll let me, and if I can get out of this building without being arrested.

TWENTY-NINE
WEDNESDAY 4PM

Getting out of the building was the easy part once Charlie realised that there were four sets of stairs, all leading to a different outside door. The rain had eased, and Charlie found a cab dropping a mother, three small children and a mountain of suitcases off by the street entrance. He helped unload the cases and asked the driver to take him to the hospital.

———

THE MAN TALKING to Orianna in the waiting room outside Intensive Care looked so like Tom that Charlie drew in a breath and almost spoke. But Tom would never wear those clothes, and the man's hair and beard were grey where Tom's were dark and full. Like Tom, the man looked kind, but Charlie detected a weakness and a slowness about him that said he would wait for someone else to make the decisions. Should he wait for Orianna to introduce them? It was too late. The man had seen him. Charlie stepped forward.

"Mr Pennant? My name is Charlie Rees. Tom's partner."
He held out his hand.

Gordon Pennant moved in Charlie's direction, automatically polite, and opened his mouth to speak. Then a woman came through the archway to the waiting room.

"I don't think so, Gordon," she said. "Please leave, whoever you are."

Charlie felt her words like a blow. He dropped his hand.

"I have come to see Tom," he said with the remains of his composure. "I am sure Orianna has explained that Tom and I live together."

The woman's face showed contempt: chin down, lips curling.

"Orianna," she said in the tone of voice that meant *despicable*.

"Verity, please. Orianna is the mother of our granddaughters." The man sounded as if it was something he had said many times before.

"*Ann* is the mother of Amelia and Zenobia," Verity spat out. Orianna visibly flinched, muttered *their names are Amelie and Ziggy*, and Charlie saw her hands curl into fists. She took a deep breath and let it out slowly.

"Mrs Pennant," Charlie said, "I have come to see Tom."

She turned away from her husband. "You have no right to see my son. You can leave now, or I can call the hospital security. Or perhaps the police. Because I think the police wish to talk to you, but frankly I have better things to do. Gordon, the consultant is on his way."

"Wait. Please." Charlie felt himself losing his composure, in the full knowledge that he *must* keep his anger under control. "Tom would want me here."

"*Tomos*," she said with emphasis, "is seriously ill. He may not recover. He needs his *family*, not someone who ran away when he was shot. Leave."

A hand gripped Charlie's arm. "Charlie," Orianna said into his ear, "There's no point." She held on to him as Tom's parents walked away. "There's no point," she repeated. "No one has ever won an argument with Verity Pennant, and the longer Tom is in the coma, the worse she gets. She'll call the cops if you stay, just out of spite, because that's what she's like."

Charlie hadn't eaten or slept properly since the shooting. He was keeping going not on fumes, but on the memory of fumes. He felt every molecule of his body being drawn thinner and thinner with the pretense that he could function.

Compared to the thought of losing Tom, the possibility of arrest bothered Charlie not at all. The only reason to avoid it was the need to see Tom before ... he was not going to think that.

"I didn't run away," he said.

"You saved Tom's life," Orianna answered. "I didn't know what to do, and you did. But you'll never persuade Verity, and she wouldn't care anyway."

Maybe Charlie had run away. If he hadn't wanted to stop the gunman, maybe Tom wouldn't have been shot. Maybe this *was* his fault for wanting to be a hero. Tom had saved Orianna, and instead of saving Tom, Charlie had forgotten about everything but his stupid *job*. It must have shown on his face.

"Stop it, Charlie. Stop thinking about it. Come and have a coffee, and something to eat. I need to talk to you." She pulled at his sleeve.

"I don't want coffee. I want to see Tom."

"That's not going to happen while his mother is in this mood. I'll talk to Gordon before I go."

"Go where?"

"That's what I want to talk to you about."

THE HOSPITAL HAD every fast-food outlet Charlie had ever heard of, and some he hadn't. The food court was vast and crowded. Orianna must have recognised the impossibility of Charlie making any kind of choice. She led him to a railed seating area by a bakery, and half pushed him into a nearby sofa. By the time she got back, he was struggling to keep his eyes open. The tray of food included a boxed salad, sandwiches and doughnuts along with large cups of coffee. Charlie couldn't summon up enthusiasm for any of it.

"You are making yourself ill," Orianna said. "That won't help Tom. I want you to eat, and then book yourself into a hotel so you can sleep. It isn't up for discussion."

She was right, he knew she was right. He couldn't think straight, and his limbs drooped with weariness. He reached for a sandwich.

Between them they emptied the tray. Charlie felt overfull and bloated afterwards, but he supposed he would feel better after a sleep.

"The thing is, Charlie, I want to go home. I'm going to change my flights and go as soon as I can. It's not that I want to leave you and Tom. You need to know that."

"Why then?" Charlie couldn't process what he was hearing. All he could think about was that without Orianna, he had no chance of seeing Tom, or even finding out how he was.

"I'm frightened," Orianna said simply. "You think the shooter was after Kaylan but what if you're wrong? Even you said one of those threats against me was credible. Dana has been threatened too, and last night someone tried to set fire to the bookstore. If I could do something for Tom, I'd stay, but I can't ... The girls are already facing the loss of their father. I can't risk them losing me too if there's a nutcase after me. I'm so sorry, Charlie, but I need to be at home." She put her head in her hands and began to cry softly.

There was no point in arguing about it. Her mind was made up.

"I'm not leaving," Charlie said. "I am going to see Tom and then I'm going to prove that Kaylan was the target. End of story."

Charlie watched Orianna walk away. They'd embraced, and Charlie had pretended to understand why she wanted to leave and tried not to think about her saying *the girls already risk losing their father*. Because the girls' father was his Tom, and the thought of losing Tom was ... not something he could admit as a possibility. He put his elbows on the table and rested his head in his hands, eyes closed. The noise of the food court seemed to get louder: American voices, the hiss of a coffee machine, the clatter of dropped cutlery somewhere behind a counter. The smells were of coffee and sugar and he could taste them both on his tongue. His eyes were irritated and raw from lack of sleep; he rubbed at them as if that would improve things, feeling dried-hard salt from his tears in his eyelashes. God, but he was a mess. Bits of the song *Englishman in New York* ran through his head again. Yes, he was an alien. Didn't understand how things worked here, didn't know who he could trust, and following his instincts had led to disaster. If he hadn't run after the gunman ... He wanted the familiar sight of trees on the hills and mountains in the distance, not these endless canyons of streets with their wide pavements, strange shops and people shouting and shuffling. He longed for the familiar sounds of people speaking Welsh and the voices of his friends and colleagues. No wonder Orianna wanted to go home.

Tom

Was Charlie dead? Had he been shot, too? Tom couldn't
remember. The voices were still there, disturbing him, making
demands when all he wanted was to be still and calm. He
didn't want to look up at the light at the top of the water — it
looked attractive, but he had an idea that looks could be decep-
tive. And if Charlie wasn't there, did he want to go? It would be
easier to stay here and wait for the lights to go out altogether.
He thought it probably wouldn't take long, and he could spend
the time drifting and remembering how it had been. Him and
Charlie. How they met. His growing understanding that
Charlie was the person for him. Charlie's courage. The way
Charlie walked into danger because it was the right thing to do.
The feeling of Charlie's skin against his own. Charlie laughing.
The images of Charlie dissolved and Tom saw that he was back
in the bookshop with Orianna and Charlie. The shooting
started again, and Tom saw Charlie move.

He ran towards the gunman. Did he get killed?

"Where is Charlie?" he asked, though he didn't think it came out right. "Where is Charlie?" he asked again. Because when he spoke, even through the weight of water, the voices started up again and he could listen. He listened but none of the voices were Charlie. He closed his eyes against the light and floated in the darkness. Swimming up through the water would be hard work, and he was so tired. The soft darkness embraced him gently, pulling him away from the surface, and he let it happen.

Charlie

Charlie watched the TV without enthusiasm. It was tuned to a rolling news station: someone in the studio, someone else on location and a ribbon across the bottom of the screen. Suddenly the words *Blue Wave Books* caught his eye.

Victim of Blue Wave Books shooting dies in hospital bringing the number of dead to three. The victim has not been named at this time. NYPD say the investigation is ongoing and complex. Press conference later. The New York Yankees...

TOM. Tom had died and no one had told him.

HERE, in this hospital, a few corridors away from Charlie, who loved him, who would have begged him to live and comforted him if he couldn't. And now Charlie felt nothing. Just a gaping hole where his life used to be. A hole filled with *what ifs*. What if he hadn't chased the gunman? What if he had been quicker with the tourniquet? What if he had forced his way into Tom's room? What if he had said no to the New York trip? What if they had sat somewhere else in the bookshop? What if...?

At the edges of his consciousness, Charlie felt the swell of a tsunami of grief and loss. If he let himself go, he would be overwhelmed in an instant. He couldn't bear it, couldn't face it, wasn't ready. His jaw hurt from the effort of holding back the tide of pain, and his heart felt heavy in his chest. His arms wrapped round himself when he wanted Tom's arms, wanted Tom. Tom's old leather jacket was in the bag on his lap, but he couldn't move to put it on. The pain got behind his eyes and into his throat, but he didn't give in. If he thought about living in a world without Tom, grief would swallow him whole and spit out the pieces.

Because there had never been anyone who had *seen* Charlie as Tom had. No one stopped Charlie's heart the way Tom did. Charlie thought of Tom's eyes, and the way his eyes and hands moved together as he drew. Tom's pencil made marks on paper like his hands made marks on Charlie's skin. Now those marks were etched, as if Charlie had been dipped in an acid bath, the acid stripping everything away except the marks Tom made. That was all Charlie was. The marks Tom had made. The scream began to force its way out of Charlie's chest, and he stood up needing somewhere private to let it out.

He ran blindly toward the nearest bathroom, tears obscuring his vision. In the entrance, a cleaners cupboard stood open, mops and buckets stacked against the wall. Charlie threw himself inside and closed the door behind him, sank to the floor and let go of his self-control.

All he could think of was Tom. Tom in his red lumberjack shirt, Tom naked on his knees in front of Charlie, Tom in his suit, in his beautiful office, Tom with his children. All the plans they were making. The trips they discussed. The places Tom wanted to visit in New York. The way they were going to grow old together. The proposed exhibition of Tom's drawings of Charlie. All gone as if they had never been. A future that wasn't going to happen. Charlie left here, on his own with a future he couldn't face, didn't want to acknowledge, couldn't bear. He put his head down and let the tears flow silently, washing away all his dreams. The ache in his face wasn't the bruises anymore. It was the pain of loss.

The door opened behind him and he fell into the light. A man in overalls looked down at Charlie.

"You lose someone, my friend?" he asked and Charlie had never heard such kindness. He couldn't answer but he didn't need to. "Let's get you somewhere better than this," the man said, and stooped down to help Charlie to his feet. He hugged Charlie and Charlie wanted to cling to this stranger, except the stranger wasn't the body he wanted to cling to. And that was another loss, the loss of the body that felt like home, and Charlie didn't think he could survive any more.

"Charlie! Oh my God, Charlie." He felt soft hands pulling him into an embrace, soft hair falling over his face. He heard Orianna whisper, "Thank you," and footsteps fade.

"Tom," Charlie said. "I want to see Tom."

THIRTY-ONE

WEDNESDAY 5PM

Orianna hugged Charlie close, stroking his hair like Tom would have done.

"Let's see what I can do," she said.

"It hardly matters now," Charlie sobbed. "They surely won't stop me seeing him now."

Orianna pulled back and looked Charlie in the face, taking in the bruises and his tear-stained cheeks. "Charlie, what's happened? Why are you so upset? Tom is the same, and unfortunately, so are his horrible parents."

"He died, Ori. Tom's dead. It was on the news."

Orianna stared at him, then using a strength he wasn't aware she possessed, turned him round physically to face the TV on the wall.

At that moment a face appeared on the TV screen. "Bookstore Shooting Victim Named as English Literature Professor Curtis Washington."

The relief knocked the legs from under him. He collapsed into his chair as the TV picture changed to a woman standing next to a police officer. There was no sound — the space was too noisy — but the scrolling text asked for privacy for Professor Washington's family at this difficult time. The police officer led the woman away from the cameras. Charlie knew how she felt, and it tore open the last of his defences.

The scene shifted to the outside of the bookshop. Floral tributes lay underneath the police tape. The front window had been boarded up. Tears flowed down his face, and he couldn't find the energy to care who saw. He cried for the bereaved woman, and for her family. He cried for Tom, who didn't deserve this, and maybe even for Kaylan who had been murdered in cold blood. And he cried for himself for the first time. He let himself *feel* the fear of losing Tom, and made no attempt to hide from his terror. He knew what he had to do.

CHARLIE DIDN'T BOTHER TRYING to talk to Tom's parents, or waiting to see if Orianna was following. He went to the nurses' station and simply demanded access to Tom.

"I have waited," he said. "I'm done waiting. I saved his life and I love him and when he comes round, I'm going to ask him to marry me. I don't care if you take me in there in handcuffs, between two security guards, but I *am* going to see him."

The charge nurse mumbled something about *family only*.

Charlie leaned over the desk. "I thought we'd done with this shit over AIDS. Who has his medical insurance card? His parents, who he hasn't seen for years, or the man he lives with? Who is his emergency contact? Who lives at the same address? Define *family*."

A middle-aged woman in scrubs took Charlie's arm. "I'll take him," she said, and pulled Charlie back toward the exit to the ward and to Tom's room. "You need to talk to him, honey. He's losing the fight, and no amount of his mother's bullying is going to bring him back. She's got everyone on the ward shaking in their shoes, but that's not what your man needs."

Verity Pennant started arguing before Charlie was even through the door. He ignored her. Tom's eyes were closed. They seemed to have sunk back into his head, dark shadows covering his cheeks like the bruises covered Charlie's face.

"Tom," Charlie said quietly in Welsh. "Tomos Dylan. Do not even *think* about fucking dying. I need you to wake up, lovey. There's something I want to ask you."

Charlie thought Tom's eyelids might have fluttered but he couldn't be sure. Verity's bad temper was filling the room. Charlie asked, "Please could you leave us alone?"

The same nurse who had brought Charlie in, put her hand on Verity's arm. She shook it off angrily. But she went to the door.

"Five minutes," she said. "Five minutes and then you're out."

"Just fuck off," Charlie whispered.

This time when Tom's eyelids fluttered, Charlie was sure. He talked. He told Tom how much he loved him, how much his daughters needed him. "And even that bloody art school needs you, Tom. And I want to ask you to marry me, but I can't unless you wake up."

"Yes," said a croaky voice from the bed.

"Jesus, Tom, I thought you were dead. You bastard, I thought you were dead." Charlie's body shook uncontrollably, and tears of relief spurted unchecked from his eyes.

"Not dead," Tom said. It sounded like speaking was an effort. His eyes stayed closed.

Charlie grabbed the hand without the drip and squeezed.

"Please wake up, Tom."

"Don't go. Don't die, Charlie. You ran at the gunman. I saw.

Don't die, Charlie." Charlie squeezed Tom's hand even harder and felt the same squeeze around his heart.

Orianna burst into the room.

"He's awake. Sort of." Charlie said. "You'd better get a nurse."

Tom's breathing appeared to slow down and Charlie was trying to control his panic when the door opened again and one of the more pleasant doctors came in, closely followed by Tom's parents.

"He woke up," Charlie said, "but ..."

The doctor looked at Tom, and at all the machines, bleeping in the background.

"He's asleep," he said. "Normal sleep. Not in a coma any more. But he's got a lot of recovery to do, and he'll need rest. I think it's time you all left."

"No," Charlie said. "I'm staying."

The doctor shrugged. Charlie saw his name was Dr Graeme Cheetah, which seemed somehow familiar. Verity opened her mouth to begin speaking, and the doctor said, "Best leave it for now. Your son needs quiet."

"I should be with him," Verity hissed. "Not this ... person."

Charlie turned round. "*This person* is Tom's fiancé. I asked him to marry me and he said yes. Which I think gives me the right to stay, don't you?"

"Let's leave them to it," Orianna said and took Verity's elbow to lead her out of the room. The doctor plucked the medical chart from its holder on the end of the bed, and stood with it, pen in hand, looking expectantly at Orianna and the Pennants. They left, Verity still protesting.

Dr Cheetah made a few notes on the chart.

"Is that true?" he asked Charlie. "Tom woke up for long enough to accept your proposal?"

Charlie nodded. Because that was what that "yes" had meant, he was sure of it.

"Fine. But you need to know that the police are looking for you. I don't know what you've done, but I think you should probably leave too, unless you want to get married in handcuffs."

Grand Central station was packed, and though Charlie knew it would be chock full of CCTV cameras, he felt safe there. He didn't think it was somewhere Special Agent Mead and his cohorts would look for him. He wanted to be in Tom's over-heated room, with Tom, but that *was* somewhere the FBI could find him easily. When he had thought Tom was dead, being arrested hadn't mattered. Now it did.

He'd considered various places he could hide in the hospital and rejected them all. Maybe he would try to sneak in at night, but that might be what Mead would expect him to do. In the meantime, he would wait for Unwin's call here, where he could get coffee and enough cake to sink a ship. He loved everything about the station from the warm buff-coloured walls to the entrances to the different tracks with their crown-like carvings and the little Art Deco-style lights. It felt like a place where anything could happen and probably did.

The choice of places to eat almost defeated him. Many of them seemed to offer the same or similar food items: made-up baked goods like cronuts or cinnamon bites; things employing sourdough bread, and, of course, pizza. Some focused on their coffee. Others offered juices and still others, tea. After wandering for twenty minutes, Charlie chose at random and ordered coffee and a cinnamon roll. He thought he probably looked ridiculous in his baseball cap and dark glasses, but the barista took his money with a smile. Once he relaxed enough to look around at people rather than food options, he realised than plenty of them were as oddly dressed as him.

Disentangling social classes was hard here in New York. At home, he could have told who was on their way to or from work, who was on holiday, who going home after a day's shopping or heading out for a meal with friends. Here, trainers and sweatpants were ubiquitous. He wondered where the men in expensive suits were, and the women in high end fashion. It was something he would have discovered if he and Tom had finished their holiday. Because they wouldn't have spent all their time in Central Park or in bed. Probably.

The phone rang and it was Unwin.

"Andrew Dwyer. Interesting character."

"I know that, Unwin, mate. *How* is he interesting exactly?"

"In no particular order, then. He's probably broke, he's a major league Donald Trump supporter, his business is formally construction, but informally, protection rackets and illegal fights. It is nowhere suggested that the former president is aware of any of these less savoury activities. He appears to have political ambitions, though exactly what those ambitions are is not stated; there is just a lot of talk about his desire to serve the public, which I understand to be code for *Vote For Me.*"

"Political ambition and being broke don't go hand-in-hand. Nor does being broke and being a mate of Donald Trump. And the last I heard, protection and illegal fights tend to be lucrative."

"Which is all interesting, right?" There was a pause.

"Thing is, Dwyer had this swanky office downtown, and now he doesn't. He has a post office box giving a swanky address, but no physical presence there, just a mail drop."

"So, the lease expired on his offices, and he couldn't get anything new? Like in Trump Tower? Do they have offices in Trump Tower?"

"No idea. But the old office is still empty. It's been advertised, but no takers. And like I say, Dwyer has no office."

Charlie suspected that Dwyer did have an office and that he'd seen it — the temporary one at the building site.

"This shortage of money? Sudden crash or a slow drain?" Charlie asked. He was fairly certain that Unwin would be following the same train of thought as him.

"You mean, did Kaylan steal all Dwyer's cash?"

"The thought had occurred to me."

"There's no way of knowing. I haven't had time to do a deep dive into Dwyer's finances, but it's suggestive. If Dwyer pissed Kaylan off, well, we both know how Kaylan gets his revenge."

Charlie thought that idea fitted well with the way Dwyer had sprung to Kaylan's defence. Because what Dwyer had been saying was that Charlie should not look at Kaylan's behaviour or investigate his death. Had Kaylan stolen the money Dwyer was relying on to further his political ambitions, and spent it on a stunning million-dollar apartment? If so, and if Dwyer had killed his nephew, then he wasn't going to want Charlie poking his nose in. If what he suspected was true, then Charlie thought he was very lucky not to be wearing concrete boots at the bottom of the Hudson River. But if Dwyer had moved his office to the building site rather than some expensive skyscraper office with a doorman and a million security cameras, then going and checking it out for evidence was a possibility...

"Sarge." Patsy's voice interrupted Charlie's chain of

thought. "This Dwyer sounds like a piece of shit, but a dangerous piece of shit. Like with guns and a bunch of cage fighters on tap."

"Your point is?"

"My point is that Eddy is acting sergeant while you're away, and he's crap, and they've sent a right idiot to make up the numbers. We need you to come back, not finish up sleeping with the fishes."

"Sleeping with the fishes?" Charlie said. "Who says *sleeping with the fishes?*"

The same people who say "Wearing concrete boots at the bottom of the Hudson River," that's who.

There was something about Dwyer that set alarm bells ringing on both sides of the Atlantic. He would be stupid to ignore the noise. If Tom had to stay alive for him, then surely Charlie owed it to Tom to stay alive too. Breaking into the site office was tempting but it was also the equivalent of poking an angry bear with a short stick.

"Trust me," Charlie said, "and be kind to Eddy."

Charlie bolstered himself with more coffee. He needed to think and he felt the need to write things down. That, more than anything else, told him how exhausted he was. Usually, he would lean back in his chair in the ridiculously dark office and let the thoughts do their own thing while Patsy and Eddy squabbled in the outer room. Then it would be down to the whiteboard with the coloured pens to see if his thoughts still made sense when he shared them with the others. Now, every thought seemed to skitter away from him before he could catch it and let it interact with everything else. He felt in his pockets for a pen, and came up blank. What he did find was a small sketchbook with a propelling pencil attached to it by a piece of elastic in Tom's messenger bag. Charlie flicked through, not surprised to find it full of tiny but exquisite drawings. He saw that most of them were of himself, and a couple of them were not something he would have wanted his mother or his work colleagues to see. He grinned to himself, wondering when Tom had made those particular sketches ... It felt mildly sacrilegious to turn to a blank page and make notes about crime.

He put the word Kaylan in the centre of the page, realising that he was taking extra care to form his letters, because it was Tom's book. Tom would have drawn a tiny picture of Kaylan's face, then sinuous arrows to show connections between the different players — who would have been represented with a quick sketch. Charlie had watched Tom drawing without apparently even looking at the page, often creating fantastical monsters with the faces of people he knew. By contrast, Charlie would be sticking to mundane words, and his connecting arrows, if there were any, would be merely crooked.

He arranged the names around the paper: Dwyer, Special Agents Mead and Bart, Sabrina Sully, Sully Cybersecurity, "Special Agent" Brody Murphy. Then he added himself. Finally, and with a little grin, Former President Donald Trump. Tom would have added a ridiculous wave of hair to the letters, so Charlie did the same. It didn't look like hair, but it didn't matter. It brought Tom into the exercise with him and made him feel warm and fuzzy.

God, I am such a sap when it comes to that man. Get back to work.

He added the words Grandmother (legacy?), Vitruvius and Llanfair College, then (the fake) Deganway and his mother. Finally, he started drawing arrows. Most of the arrows converged on Kaylan and he added dollar signs to them all, except his own. Kaylan had stolen from them all. Everyone on the page, except Brody Murphy and the two FBI agents. But the two agents were investigating cybercrime, and it didn't come much more cybercrime than Kaylan's activities. He hadn't stolen directly from Donald Trump, but if Dwyer was serious about getting into politics, it was going to cost him in terms of big campaign donations.

Charlie looked at what he'd done. He needed another colour, and scrabbled around in the messenger bag, releasing the smell of Old Spice, until he came up with one of those four-colour ballpoint pens he remembered from his childhood. Quite why Tom should have such a thing, Charlie didn't know. All the colours seemed to work, because *of course* he had to test them all. And he realised that he was enjoying himself working out the puzzle. Now he had spoken to Tom, the clouds had lifted. Yes, he was still exhausted and yes, he was going to have to keep moving, and no, it wouldn't be easy to prove his innocence, but he could do it now that he knew Tom was going to get better.

Charlie drew another set of arrows around Andrew Dwyer. Dwyer connected to Kaylan and to himself and to Brody Murphy.

Finally, he added Orianna. She had an arrow to him, and one to Brody Murphy, and to Deganway's wall of pictures, but it was messy. No obvious cause and effect. Charlie remembered a lecture from Freya Ravensbourne, his immediate boss about Occam's Razor. *If there are two theories pointing to the same result, the simpler one is better.* Orianna as a potential victim *sounded* plausible, except as Charlie had pointed out several times, *she wasn't dead.* Kaylan was dead. As a gay man, Charlie was all too aware of how easily ideology turned to violence. But he'd been a policeman for a long time too, and he truly believed that the love of money was the root of much evil. Kaylan was a thief and a damn good one. The list of his victims was long.

The page filled with more arrows in different colours, and scribbles showing relationships until it was a jumble of writing, smeared ink blobs and pencil. But Charlie could see the way forward. He just had to keep himself out of the hands of the police for long enough to pull it off — which would be easy if he could just stay here in Grand Central Station eating cinnamon buns. Rather, he was going to have to go out into the city, find people who didn't want to see him and tell them a lot of lies. Convincingly.

He drew circles around a couple of names, and leaned back in the chair, the babble around him becoming white noise. He put his hand up to his face, feeling the stubble on his chin and cheeks, being careful not to press too hard on the bruises. There was no need to look down at his clothes to know that they had been though some hard times and were showing the marks. If he was going visiting, he needed to be cleaner and smarter. Tom would put up with sweaty, scruffy Charlie, and love him, but everyone else would take a bit more work. Clothes, shower, sleep, lies. In that order.

THIRTY-FOUR
WEDNESDAY SOMETIME

Tom

No matter how hard he tried, Tom could not manage to return himself to the dreamy underwater place where he had spent the last ... however long. Instead of the warm and welcoming depths, he was stuck with bright and flashing lights, hard surfaces and pain. Worst of all, no Charlie. Charlie had been there, he knew, but he wasn't here now. Just his parents, whom he hadn't seen for literal years, and who looked the same but older. His mother was, if anything, more strident and demanding than he remembered, and his father more melancholy.

The nurses were kind and the doctors businesslike. Everyone kept telling him how ill he had been, as if that was supposed to mean something. He had no memory of being ill, though he certainly felt ill enough now. He wanted to object to the lack of dignity afforded by catheterisation, the drip keeping him fed and hydrated and the sticky pads on his chest. He felt as if he were on show to every passer-by, without the privacy to pee or brush his own teeth.

And his mother. Oh God, his mother. If anyone else told him that *she means well*, he would scream and to hell with all the needles and machines. She let slip that Orianna had been there, but when he demanded to see her, was told she had gone home *to Amelia and Zenobia*. That's when he told her to go.

"We both know the girls' names," he said. "I don't know why you keep pretending they are called something else. It's time you went home too. I'm sure you have your own patients to bully."

Her outburst was as expected, but promotion to college principal had given him the confidence to say what he thought in words as much as with a pencil on paper.

"I live with a man. His name is Charlie Rees and he's a policeman, a detective. He's my family. Charlie, A to Z, Ann and Orianna. People who like me as I am. So, thank you both for coming, but please go home." He closed his eyes, and she took the hint.

His father came in some time later, and tried to smooth things over. But Tom was tired, and in pain, and just wanted someone to come and give him some of the good drugs, the ones that would send him back to oblivion, because reality was horrible. He told his father that he was wasting his time.

"You've had years to make things right, and you couldn't be bothered. It's too late."

Charlie

When Charlie came out of the station it was to the return of the rain. Torrents of rain. So much rain that he couldn't see from one side of the street to the other. Rain bouncing off the pavement, forming lakes on the road, filling the air with the smell of water. The streets were a sea of umbrellas, so many that Charlie should have been able to stay dry without one of his own. Except the rain was too heavy; even with umbrellas, everyone was wet. He remembered seeing a couple of stores that he thought would sell him what he needed when he and Tom had been to stare at the Empire State Building, so he put his head down and set off.

This part of the city was crowded, a steady stream of people entering and leaving, closing and opening their umbrellas as they walked in and out of the shops. Charlie caught sight of himself in a mirror in his chosen clothes store. His hair was dark and flattened by the rain despite the baseball cap. His trousers clung to his thighs where the rain had soaked through and though his jacket had done remarkably well, his shirt was wet and see-though. The trainers Murphy had bought him were saturated. Even after finger-combing his wet hair in front of a mirror, he looked weary beyond imagining.

Half an hour later he had everything he needed, from boxers and socks outward, all the way to a new red padded jacket. There was a respectable-looking hotel directly across the street, so once he was sure his packages would survive the rain, he ran with the hope they had a room. They did, and though the phrase *sticker shock* applied, he paid cheerfully — with one of Tom's cards. Luckily, a large and noisy party entered the hotel behind Charlie, distracting the receptionist from looking too closely at the picture on Tom's ID.

The room was just large enough for a double bed, a chair and desk, and a bedside table on each side of the bed. The view was of the wall of an airshaft about four feet from his own window. But it had a walk-in shower, a bed and no one knew where he was. Showering off the sweat and grime was wonderful. Climbing between the clean sheets was better. If he put Tom's jacket on the pillow next to him so that he could smell Tom, there was no one to see. He slept as if drugged, and woke ten hours later, ready to start telling lies, or in one case, the truth.

THIRTY-FIVE

THURSDAY 8AM

There was no kettle or coffee maker in Charlie's hotel room but he remembered there was one in the lobby. He dressed quickly and went to collect the strongest brew he could get. There were muffins too and he helped himself. There would be time for real food later. Back in his room he got out Tom's sketchbook opened to the pages of scribbled names and arrows. It wasn't his beloved Llanfair whiteboard, but it was the best substitute he had. It had shown him a pattern last night. Did it still show a pattern? He decided that it did, or possibly it showed more than one. If he was wrong, he would be putting himself in the line of fire — again — but he didn't think he was wrong. He picked up his phone and sent a text to Mal Kent.

CHARLIE REES: ***Could you call me, please?***

THEN HE TOOK a deep breath and waited. Less than a minute later the phone rang.

"Thank you for ringing, sir." Charlie took another deep breath. "I was wondering if you could get a message to the FBI? I'm certain I can get a confession from Kaylan's killer, but I need them to witness it so I'm off the hook."

"I'm listening, Charlie. Even though I'm still dealing with your last request. But first, how's Tom?"

"Awake. I think he'll be out of intensive care soon. But the doctors have warned me off. Say the police are waiting for me to show up. So, I have to get this warrant dropped. Because I want to see him." The last words came out in a rush. Charlie knew that Kent had contacts everywhere. He went to conferences, led training sessions, welcomed visitors and still managed to ensure Clwyd Police had the best clear-up rate in Wales. But Charlie had to convince him that setting himself up like a sacrificial lamb would work.

"It's all about money, sir. Kaylan has been stealing right, left and centre. I think he's stolen from his uncle, Andrew Dwyer, and Dwyer wants his money back. Dwyer is a gangster with political ambitions, and some legitimate businesses."

"You know this, how?"

Not a question Charlie wanted to answer. "Easy to find out about Dwyer. He doesn't hide his ambitions."

There was a short pause.

"If I am understanding you, Charlie, you are going to tell Dwyer you can get his money back from the now sadly deceased Kaylan, and you want me to ensure the FBI are there when he confesses to murder? Even though you can't in fact, give Dwyer his money back, and you have no reason to suppose Dwyer will confess anyway."

That was a horribly accurate summary of Charlie's plan. Or mostly.

But Kent hadn't finished. "Just because Dwyer wants his

money back doesn't mean he killed Kaylan. Surely, he's less likely to get the money with Kaylan dead?"

"Kaylan doesn't work by normal rules, sir. Sorry, didn't. He stole from people he'd finished with, or who he was angry with. Sure, he spent the money — he bought a million-dollar apartment here. But he stole as a kind of punishment. He was never going to give Dwyer his money back, and he could easily have done more damage. His father's business collapsed because of him. Kaylan was a liability. And the whole family is gun-crazy. Kaylan managed to get a gun in the UK and shoot me. If I was Andrew Dwyer and I'd pissed Kaylan off, I wouldn't be feeling very safe. Maybe Kaylan had threatened to start stealing from Dwyers's political cronies." It was possible, and exactly the sort of thing Kaylan would do. "He was impulsive, and he never much cared what damage he did. He got obsessed with an idea and nothing else mattered until — as he saw it — he got let down. And he's only twenty. Not exactly mature."

"Where's the evidence that Dwyer fitted this pattern?"

"He's part of Kaylan's family. Everything I know about Kaylan says he hates his family and will do anything to hurt them. That's why he came to Wales. The reputational damage Kaylan did to his dad's firm meant his mother had to move, and depend on Dwyer for financial support. Robbing Dwyer would hurt his mother too. Like I said, he's a kid acting out. Thinking things through isn't— wasn't something he did."

Charlie was clenching his jaw in his effort to persuade Kent to see it. Kaylan had watched his friend die and done nothing to help. Once you knew that about Kaylan, you stopped expecting him to behave in any way that made sense.

"Okay then. Suppose I'm with you thus far. Why haven't US law enforcement reached the same conclusion as you?"

"Because US law enforcement brought a psychopath out of a British jail so he could, I dunno, hack into Russian government computers. And if that tidbit of information was widely shared, US law enforcement wouldn't look very good in the media. Alternatively, the FBI thought they could control Kaylan, and the reality turned out to be less than optimal. Like trying to control a toddler by asking nicely."

"It's possible that they don't want any light shining on Kaylan. You think they started off with the hate-crime stuff to divert attention—but you were making too much noise, so they started harassing you?" Kent asked. "I did tell you to leave it alone."

"Yes, sir, you did." More than once.

"And if I somehow manage to get a message to the people who are trying to arrest you for murder, what will you do?"

"Then I will get a message to Andrew Dwyer, inviting him to collect information about how to get his money back."

"Do you have that information, Charlie?" Kent asked, though Charlie suspected he knew the answer.

"No, sir, but I *have* searched Kaylan's flat, and Dwyer doesn't know I *didn't* find anything. And Dwyer probably knows that Kaylan stole from the art college, so I think I can convince him we're on the same side. Or at least for long enough that he doesn't kill me."

"I'll ring you back," Kent said and ended the call.

THIRTY-SIX

THURSDAY 10AM

Charlie dressed with care for his visit to Sabrina Sully. He decided against shaving because the stubble covered up the worst of the bruises — just trimmed the edges a bit, so that it looked deliberate. He donned the dark glasses, and at first glance, he didn't look like the victim of a beating. He was clean, tidy and smelled of soap. It would have to do. A bus took him from mid-town up the west side of the park. Sabrina's apartment building was on a quiet street. He looked around for a car park attached to the building, but if there was one, he couldn't see it. The street was filled with parked cars, and there were plenty of black SUVs. He didn't have time to take a close look at each of them — he had lies to tell, so he pressed the buzzer for Sabrina's flat. Sabrina let him in without comment, and as before led him to the balcony. It was much cooler than on his last visit, so he kept his coat on. Sabrina didn't appear to feel the chill. She was in athletic clothes, looking well rested, fit and toned, still showing no signs of grief.

"Mrs Sully," he began, "I would like to talk to you about Kaylan's bank accounts."

"Oh, yes? I can't pretend I don't need the money. His grandmother's inheritance you know. It should have come to me of course. It was far too much money for a teenager and he used it to hurt me and his father. I don't know how I came to have such a selfish child, but of course that doesn't mean I didn't love him. No mother should have to go through what I've been through ..."

When she paused to take a breath, Charlie said, "I have an idea that Kaylan may have borrowed some money from your brother, Andrew Dwyer."

"My brother has been a saint, an absolute saint. He's very well-connected. Politically. A close friend of President Trump. A *close* friend. We need more like him, but instead we're getting all this wokeness, and rainbow flags and our children being corrupted. It's disgusting what this country has come to."

Did she really believe this stuff, or was it a defence mechanism for trying to cope with the mess her life had become? All Charlie knew for sure was that Sabrina was consistent, so her next topic would be immigrants. It was and he tuned her out until she paused for breath again.

"I think I may be able to get your brother's money back if he's prepared to act quickly. Once the FBI or the police find out, all the accounts will be frozen."

"Isn't that typical? The federal government has no business interfering in people's private affairs, but that's never stopped it. Of course, Andrew wants his money back, though I'd be very interested to know how you know about it."

"I visited your son in prison in the UK," Charlie said. It was true, though had no bearing on anything they were discussing today. Happily, Sabrina took the bait.

"He should never have been in prison in the first place. He should have been sent straight home. That art school was a disaster for Kaylan. They should have refused his money and he should have gone to work for his father. That professor turned his head with communist ideas. His father was in cyber-security. The company is still going, but it's nothing without Roger. Nothing."

Charlie nodded his head. Reasoning with Sabrina would be a waste of effort. All he needed was to get the time and place of the meeting across. If she could answer a simple question as well, that would be a bonus.

"Mrs Sully, your husband was murdered outside a parking garage. The implication was that he'd driven from Chicago to New York. I'm surprised he didn't fly."

Sabrina leaned forward and looked him in the eyes. Her eyes blazed with sincerity and the muscles in her shoulders and neck stood out with the effort of communication.

"Airplanes have so many stupid, stupid, rules about guns. My husband believed in *freedom*. We need to arm ourselves against what's coming." And Sabrina was off on a diatribe against gun control. Roger Sully had driven for twelve hours so that he could bring a gun. Charlie reflected that it had done him no good at all. *Schadenfreude.* That was the word, wasn't it? Or was it *hoist by his own petard?* He still had to tell Sabrina about the meeting for Andrew Dwyer. It took him another fifteen minutes. But he thought the message had got through the cascade of words.

AS HE WALKED down the stairs and into the lobby of the apartment block, Charlie's phone buzzed with a text.

SUPT KENT: **Message passed to appropriate people. Brody Murphy will be contacting you. See him. He's legit. If the bait is not taken, I want you on the** *first available flight back here. No arguments. Be careful.*

THEN ANOTHER ONE.

SUPT KENT: **When you get back, we'll be talking about the chain of command. For now, good luck.**

CHARLIE SMILED.

CHARLIE DIDN'T NEED TELLING to be careful. He was poking the large, angry bear with a very short stick but it was the best he could do. The knowledge that he would almost certainly not face trial for murdering Kaylan Sully if he was arrested didn't make him any more inclined to risk it. He wanted to go home with Tom, not spend months in some awful New York detention complex while the wheels of justice ground on. The words *Rikers Island* sent shivers down his spine, and not in a good way. But as well as the possibility of being arrested, there was the real possibility of being shot. Everyone involved, except him, carried a gun and appeared happy to use it. He needed back-up and the only back-up he had on this side of the Atlantic was Brody Murphy. There was no need to wait for his call.

"Charlie. We need to talk," Murphy said when he answered his phone.

"When and where?"

Murphy gave Charlie the name of a coffee shop. It wasn't far from where Sabrina lived, so he set off to walk. The weather was still chilly, and rain looked like a distinct possibility but Charlie enjoyed the walk. He thought he would always like the way the city looked, or at least those bits of it he had seen — mostly Harlem, with a few excursions to Midtown and a single visit to Greenwich Village. He'd spent time in Central Park and walking up and down the fine streets on either side. He liked Harlem. It was less crowded than midtown, more open with its trees and wide streets. There were pockets of poverty but there were pockets of poverty in his apparently prosperous Welsh town. He was sorry he wouldn't be getting the chance to know the city better, because one way or another, he and Tom were going home as soon as Tom was fit to travel. Maybe they'd come back. Or maybe they'd go to Amsterdam, or Copenhagen, or Seville.

Murphy was looking at his phone when Charlie arrived. He had a bulging carrier bag on the table in front of him and when Charlie sat down, Murphy pushed the bag toward him. Charlie looked inside.

"What's this?"

"Bullet-proof vest."

Charlie raised his eyebrows. "Oh. Okay."

"It's a big risk. If it was my choice, you wouldn't be going, but I have bosses and they want it to happen. This is the best I can do."

"Then thank you."

"My bosses think you should wear a wire." Murphy produced another parcel from the seat beside him. "Drink your coffee and then we can hit the restroom so you can take your shirt off for me." He wiggled his eyebrows.

Charlie laughed. "Sorry, Brody, mate, but you aren't my

type. Plus, if you're going to feel me up, you should at least buy me dinner first."

Brody blushed neon pink.

"Okay," Charlie said. "I'll settle for a cinnamon roll. And, the thing I really need from you is the address of Dwyer's construction site. Because they took me there in a closed van, beat me up and then kicked me out in the middle of Harlem by that police station you rescued me from. I've been setting up all these meetings with no idea where the place is."

This time it was Murphy's turn to laugh. But he did tell Charlie where the construction site was.

The construction site hadn't changed since Charlie's first visit, except there was no delivery van, and so far, no thugs. He was prepared to go the whole evening without the thugs. The bruises on his face had begun to fade, but his stomach was still a million shades of dismal rainbow colours and hurt like a bitch. The bulletproof vest Murphy had loaned him dug into the bruises on his stomach every time he moved, but Charlie had promised himself and by extension, Tom, that he would be careful. Which meant that he had to come back from whatever happened tonight.

Dusk was beginning to fall when Charlie climbed on to the roof of the mobile office. He wasn't expecting anyone until much later and he wanted to be ready. Dwyer's heavies had taken him by surprise once, and it wasn't something he wanted to risk for a second time. They were an order of magnitude stronger than him, there were two of them and they had guns. If they showed up, he needed Special Agents Mead and Bart to be available to take them on.

If it all worked, the FBI would get Dwyer and Charlie

would be off the hook. He cared less about justice for Kaylan. It seemed to Charlie that Kaylan had brought his troubles on himself, although even so, he hadn't deserved to die. More importantly, nor had the two innocents who had died with him. That was Kaylan all over — he had an idea and other people suffered in the execution.

The rain continued to hold off, but the car park still smelled of mud and wet cement. The top of the office was flat, studded with rivets and painted bright yellow. Charlie's old red padded coat was unlikely to survive for much longer. It had been shredded and muddied against too many surfaces, and he was glad he had a new one waiting for him back at the hotel. But for now, it helped keep him a little bit warmer as he lay on the cold metal. He had the oddest sense that he was not alone on the construction site, even though rationally he knew he must be. He'd reconnoitered earlier and the place was deserted. Dwyer seemed to depend on the high fences and cameras to keep the area secure. The cement plant was too big to steal easily, and there were no other machines in evidence. Charlie had scrambled to look over the high wooden fence, expecting to see a building in progress. Instead, there was a large hole, half filled with dirty water. Foundation? Charlie didn't know. But he was surprised there were no machines to either make the hole bigger, or to fill it in. There were no workers or building materials either. According to Unwin, the site was going to become a modest residential tower block. Had Kaylan's thefts affected Dwyer's building programme too? He would find out when Dwyer showed up.

There were lights on tall poles around the site. They came on automatically as it got darker, illuminating the front of the offices, the cement plant and the gate. Kaylan hadn't stolen enough to get the electricity cut off at least.

First to arrive were Special Agents Mead and Bart, in a

nondescript muddy-coloured van. He could just make out Mead's features through the windscreen as they passed under one of the lights and then they parked behind the cement plant.

Charlie lay on the roof as the sky darkened. Rivets stuck into his skin and the cold seeped through his clothes but he could hear every car that passed down the street, and the voices of the pedestrians. He knew from his earlier observations that the top of the office was invisible from below.

At last, he heard the jangle of the padlock and chain and the sound of a car door opening and closing. Charlie lifted his head, knowing no one could see him in the deep shadow cast by the floodlights but still feeling as exposed as if he were naked in Times Square. He wasn't surprised to see the black SUV with the chrome fittings parked in the middle of the yard. Nor was he surprised to see Sabrina Sully climb out of it. He kept watching, expecting Dwyer to get out of the car, but Sabrina was alone. She stood in the middle of the lot peering into the dark corners. She went to the office door and rattled the handle. Charlie used the noise to cover the sound of his wriggle down from the roof. He walked round the side of the office.

"Mrs Sully. Why are you here?"

Sabrina started in alarm. "Jesus. Where did you spring from?"

"I was half expecting your brother," Charlie said.

Sabrina looked puzzled. "I don't know why. The money is all mine now." As if that was an answer to anything.

"I don't understand," Charlie said. "Did Kaylan steal from you too?"

"I don't know where my son got his money," Sabrina said with a sigh. "But as his closest relative, the money is mine. He shouldn't have been living it up in that big apartment while I depended on Andrew's charity. You told me the bank details were here, so I've come to get them. To get what's mine. Not

Andrew's, mine. Because he was my son." She gave a half shrug, as if this was self-evident.

Sabrina's blonde hair shone in the overhead lights, contrasting with her black clothes. She turned and looked at Charlie from the corner of her eyes. His blood ran cold as she produced the gun from her pocket and pointed it at him with a steady hand.

However wild her talk about money, Sabrina was a cool as a cucumber when it came to wielding a gun. "It was you, in the bookshop," he said, aiming for a similar appearance of calm. "You shot them." He could see the black-clad figure in front of him, looking at him as she looked at him now. Making the decision not to shoot him because she'd done what she came for, which was to kill her own son. He'd assumed, as everyone had, that the shooter was male. But Sabrina was tall, with wide shoulders and slim hips. Her face had been covered with a mask. All most people in the bookshop had registered was the gun in her hand.

"I should have shot you when I had the chance," she said. "But how was I supposed to know who you were?" She sounded genuinely aggrieved. She sounded like Kaylan.

Charlie hoped Sabrina decided against shooting him because they were too close for her to miss. The vest protected his chest, but that left big areas of head and body she could shoot him in. And he had *promised Tom*. He knew that to anyone watching he looked in control, and when he spoke, it was without a quaver in his voice.

"Did you kill your husband too, Mrs Sully? Was he stealing money from you as well?" The gun in her hand didn't waver.

"Politics. It was all politics. President Trump does a good job, but he's a *rich* man. He has resorts all over America and the world. I've read his books. He's *successful*. He doesn't need my money. Roger wanted to give my money away. He said the President needed funding for his campaign and if he didn't get enough to run for office again, the immigrants would take over. The last election was rigged, you know, but he'll win this time."

"But you shouldn't have to pay for it," Charlie said.

Sabrina nodded. She almost smiled. Her expression showed her relief that Charlie *understood*. But she was still pointing a gun at him. He'd spoken to her on the phone the previous year and thought her merely irritating, and that had been his impression when he spoke to her in person. Until the moment she appeared he hadn't been sure ... She was the only person who fitted the gunman's description, and she was as divorced from reality as her son, but still, he hadn't been certain.

"So, are you going to get me the bank account details?" she asked. "Because I will get the money in the end anyway. But Andrew thinks he should have some. I'd rather ... well, I think it would be better ..."

"Kaylan *stole* some of that money, Mrs Sully," Charlie said as gently as he could. "The people he stole it from are going to want it back. It might be better not to be too closely associated with stolen money."

Like I give a shit. But I really don't want to tell you I haven't the faintest idea what Kaylan did with it.

"He inherited a lot of money from his grandmother."

"I think he spent that money." *If it ever existed.*

Sabrina's face hardened, and she jerked the gun. "I want those bank account details. My son would give me the money. Are they inside the office? Have you got a key?"

"It's in my car," Charlie said. "Over there." He pointed toward the cement plant where Special Agents Mead and Bart were parked. He hoped to God that they'd heard everything Sabrina had said. If they hadn't, he was going to have to make her say it all over again. Before he could move, he heard the car doors open and the sound of shoes on gravel. It was difficult to make out the figures in the darkness, but Charlie could see them coming in their direction. As they appeared from the gloom, he saw they both had guns in their hands. Relief rolled over Charlie. He might not be armed but they were.

"Did you hear what Mrs Sully had to say?" he called as the two FBI men approached.

"We didn't need to," Mead said, and Charlie could see the look of disgust on his face as he looked at Charlie and Sabrina.

"So, you know I didn't kill anyone."

Bart laughed and mock punched his colleague. "Rees didn't kill anyone, John. Fancy that. We already *know* you didn't kill anyone, Rees. Which is not going to help you unless you help us, asshole."

Then he shot Sabrina Sully.

She fell to the ground, gun flying out of her hands, skidding across the stones and mud of the car park. Blood spurted from a wound in her chest.

"You can be next, asshole. Or you can give us the bank account details."

Two guns pointed straight at Charlie. Sabrina Sully lay on the ground crying and cursing, clutching at her chest, trying to cover the wound.

"She needs help," Charlie cried. "Call an ambulance."

"Bank accounts first," Mead said, and jerked his gun.

HE HAD GOT everything catastrophically wrong. He couldn't have been more wrong if he had tried.

Suddenly a voice boomed out of the darkness. Charlie thought it came from behind the offices, but it echoed all around so he couldn't be sure.

"FBI. Stay where you are. Drop the guns. Do it now. Drop the guns. On the ground. You're surrounded."

The voice filled the air, disconcerting Charlie, but not John Mead. He moved like lightning, grabbing Charlie before he had time to react and jabbing his gun into Charlie's neck.

"Oh, yeah?" he shouted. "You want this guy?" He started

pulling Charlie back toward the car. Bart walked backward waving his gun around.

"Special Agent Mead," came the voice. "Special Agent Bart. This is over. We have snipers. Have a look. Give it up."

Bart dropped his gun and put his hands in the air. "Don't shoot!"

Charlie didn't understand until saw the red dot move up and down Mead's arm where it grasped his body.

"They won't risk killing you. No sniper is that good. You're my ticket out of here."

Charlie let himself go limp, forcing Mead to drag him.

"On your feet, dickwad. You think I won't shoot you? I'd love to shoot you."

"You kill me, they kill you," Charlie gasped.

"Who said anything about killing?"

"I did," said Murphy from right behind them and Mead's head exploded, showering Charlie with blood and brains.

"Christ, Brody, was that really called for?" Charlie said after the rest of the hidden law enforcement personnel had revealed themselves, and an ambulance had taken Sabrina Sully away, blue lights flashing and sirens wailing. Charlie had cleaned himself as best he could and was now wearing one of the blue jackets with FBI on the back. Brody Murphy's FBI jacket to be accurate. The red coat was now red with blood and Charlie could feel blood in his hair and on his skin, despite his best efforts.

Murphy shrugged. "It was a righteous shooting," he said. "Plenty of witnesses that he was threatening you and there was no way to incapacitate him without risking your safety. I'll be on desk duty until they've investigated, but I'm not worried."

"When did you get here?" Charlie asked. "Not that I'm ungrateful, you understand."

"We've been here since I left you this morning."

"You didn't think to mention that?"

Murphy didn't answer, his eyes jerking over Charlie's shoulder to the street beyond the open gate to the yard. A familiar delivery van had slowed down by the gate, then it accelerated away.

"Shit!" Murphy yelled and ran toward Sabrina's car. Charlie ran after him and they collided by the open driver's door. The keys were in the ignition. "Drive!" Murphy commanded, and unholstered his gun as he ran round to the passenger side and leapt in. "Drive!" he yelled again. Charlie turned the key in the ignition, thanking whatever gods were listening that the car was an automatic. He'd done plenty of driving courses, but none of them had involved driving on the wrong side of the road, in the dark, in the busiest city in the world, with a companion leaning out of the passenger window trying to aim a gun at the vehicle ahead. Luckily the delivery van wasn't a high-performance vehicle, and Charlie could see it only a few hundred yards ahead. The street was four lanes wide, so he leaned on the horn and started overtaking the few cars in between. The van swerved to the right, and into a cross street as the traffic lights turned red.

"Go!" shouted Murphy.

The cross street was one way, and they were going in the wrong direction. Charlie kept the heel of his hand on the horn as he jerked the wheel from side to side, ignoring the blaring horns of the other cars, and shouts of "Asshole!" that he could hear over the squeal of tyres and the sound of cars hitting inanimate objects. He could see blue lights ahead and in his mirror and then he heard a gunshot.

"Fuck," Murphy said, and fired again. This time, his aim was better, and Charlie saw the van lurch but keep going. The sirens got louder, and blue lights swirled ahead of them at the end of the street. Over the noise of the engine, he could hear shouts of "Armed Police!" and then the crunch of the van hitting one of the cruisers setting off alarms and more shouting from the lines of police Charlie could see converging on the van.

A few seconds later, it was over, and all they could do was watch as the two thugs who'd beaten him up were handcuffed, and not gently, by uniformed NYPD officers. His stomach hurt, just looking at them, as if remembering the blows.

Cruisers blocked them in, and from the flat tyre on the back of the van, one of Murphy's shots had hit its mark. Charlie attempted to park, okay, stop within walking distance of the kerb, because he wasn't driving another yard.

"Keystone cops, much?" Charlie said to Murphy, who grinned.

"Dopamine rush. Gotta say I was hoping for Dwyer, but those two will do for starters. No need to be greedy."

"You do know I'm not insured, right? To drive this car."

"Charlie, my dear friend, that's the *least* of my problems." Murphy couldn't seem to stop smiling. "That was bizarrely fun. Do you all drive like that in Wales?"

Charlie just looked at him. The adrenaline was fading, leaving him cold and weary in his borrowed jacket.

"You are a fucking crazy man," he said.

"Back atcha. Go to the hospital and see your guy."

Charlie went, weaving his way through the tangle of police cars and FBI vans. He got a few strange looks wearing Murphy's jacket, but he was past caring. All he wanted was to see Tom, reassure himself that Tom was still alive and getting better. His legs were wobbly, and he was desperately hungry. Murphy had been swallowed up by the law enforcement personnel, so he didn't feel the need to say goodbye. He slipped unnoticed through the crowds by the parked cruisers, and on to a busier street. There he found a taxi and was soon at the nurses' station.

"How is he?" he asked the nurse who had helped him earlier, thankfully still on duty.

"He's doing really well. Better since his mother's backed off. I think he's awake. Did you know you've got blood in your hair? I think a clean-up is in order given that the last thing my patient needs is another infection."

"It's a long story," Charlie said. The nurse gave him a key and directed him to the bathroom. "Have a thorough wash and don't leave a mess."

It wasn't easy to give himself and his hair a complete wash in a small basin, but Charlie did his best. And he didn't leave a mess.

Tom wasn't only awake, he was propped up against his pillows, still attached to all the monitors, but recognisably alert and himself.

"Hi," Charlie said, and his throat blocked with emotion.

"Hi," Tom said and smiled.

Charlie leaned over and kissed him, past caring about the machines, or the likelihood of someone coming in. He pulled Tom closer as gently as he could, and felt tears well up behind his eyes.

"Come up on the bed," Tom said, moving over so that the side away from the drip had a bit of space.

Charlie took his shoes and the FBI jacket off, and sank down next to Tom, his head in the space between Tom's neck and his chest.

"I thought I would lose you," he said. "And I was so afraid."

Tom shuffled as best he could without falling off the bed so that he could look at Charlie as opposed to the ceiling. "I was just waiting for you to come and wake me up," he said. "Did I dream that you were going to ask me to marry you?"

"I do want to marry you. And you said yes."

"Good," Tom said. "But you need to know that I want a big

wedding. With a huge cake, and morning suits, and I dunno, bridesmaids or whatever, and rings and speeches. Because I want everyone to see how much I love you."

All Charlie could do was nod into Tom's beard.

"Now," Tom said, "tell me what on earth you've been doing to acquire two black eyes and a jacket with FBI on the back."

FORTY

THURSDAY MIDNIGHT

Charlie lay with his head on Tom's shoulder and tried to explain the events of the last few days. It only just made sense to him, but some things began to resolve themselves as he put them into words. "Reason suggested that there was one villain behind the whole thing, and Andrew Dwyer seemed the obvious candidate," he said.

"How come?" Tom asked.

"Well mainly because I already knew he was a gangster from what Unwin told me. Then he got his two thugs to kidnap me."

"Not because he was a Trump supporter?" Tom sounded amused. "Because I have to say, that would have been at the top of my list."

"Except they were *all* Trump supporters. All anti-gun control. Probably all homophobes. Sabrina had a thing about immigrants. But not every Trump supporter can be a criminal."

Tom snorted. "All the ones you met were."

"Small sample, but point taken." Charlie closed his eyes and let his mind wander. "The thing is, I never had time to think, never mind sleep or eat properly. I do *know* that a diet of strong coffee and doughnuts isn't optimal for thinking, but you know me and sugar. Sometimes it's the only thing I can manage ... I worried about you, all the time. To be accurate, panic is a better word than worry." He snuggled into Tom and let the peace of his presence — alive and awake — soothe him. "And even when I did get a chance to eat or sit down for a minute, those FBI bastards came and pinched my clothes, or turned up at the flat to arrest me for something. I think the only time I sat down for more than a few minutes was in the cell at the police station. If that wasn't enough, everything everyone told me was lies. Like everything. Except Kaylan's girlfriend — and she repeated the lies Kaylan had told her."

"Give me a for instance," Tom asked.

"For instance, Brody Murphy said I had met Kaylan here in New York. That was the thing about Murphy. He could tell a lie like that and sound totally convinced. I wanted to trust him, but ..."

"The reason I know you didn't meet Kaylan," Tom said, "is because I told him to get lost."

Charlie pushed himself up on his elbow. *"You met Kaylan?"*

"In that piano bar we went in. The one in Greenwich Village. I was there first because you'd stopped for something. Probably doughnuts. Or did your mother ring? I can't remember. Kaylan came in and said he wanted to talk to you. He'd recognised me and assumed I would know where you were. I told him to fuck off. We were on holiday, and the last thing we needed was reminding about the crap from last year. I got rid of him and never told you. The thing is, he said he thought his mother was trying to kill him."

"What?"

"He thought his mother was trying to kill him. Which I realise now would have been useful information."

"Sure it would. If we'd had a crystal ball to go with it. Which we didn't. He was right though. Sabrina Sully killed Kaylan and two other people. She almost certainly killed her husband. She said she was sorry she hadn't added me to the list."

The bed was far too small for both of them, but no way was Charlie moving. Talking to Tom like this was undoing all the tangles in both his mind and body. He stretched out his legs, trying to move closer. Tom smelled different, Old Spice replaced with the scent of disinfectant, but he was till Tom, and one day soon they would go home, and all this would be over ...

"So, this Andrew Dwyer character, he wasn't the villain after all?" Tom asked.

Charlie gathered his wandering thoughts. "He's certainly *a* villain. He kidnapped me for a start. But, see, like I said, everyone was lying to me. Brody Murphy let me think he was after Dwyer, when I suspect he really wanted Mead and Bart."

"Back up a bit. Remind me who Mead and Bart are. Remember, I was unconscious while all this was happening."

"Special Agent Mead and Special Agent Bart. They came to the flat after the shooting and said they were from the FBI hate crime team. They wanted us to think that the shooting was directed at Orianna and her poetry reading. Except when I looked them up, they were FBI, just cybercrimes not hate crimes."

"And your nasty suspicious mind immediately thought cybercrimes must mean Kaylan Sully, hacker extraordinaire?"

"'Xactly. I even wondered if the FBI had found out what a monster Kaylan was and shot him themselves. But I figured they were *the* FBI and probably didn't go round shooting innocent people attending a poetry reading, just to get rid of one psychopath. But Mead and Bart didn't want anyone looking at Kaylan as the main victim, and everything they did was designed to divert attention away from him."

"I'm guessing it didn't work for you?"

"Not even a bit. They wanted it all tidied away as a hate crime shooting, thoughts and prayers, too bad, so sad. Then if that didn't work, they wanted me out of the way because I wouldn't let it go."

Tom laughed. "Hard to believe." He poked Charlie very gently in the ribs, and then kissed him. "I dreamed about you," he said. "I think they gave me drugs that you probably shouldn't take for too long, but I dreamed all the time, and you were always there in my dreams." He swallowed, and Charlie saw Tom's eyes shining with unshed tears. "There was a bit... where I was, I don't know, kind of dreaming and floating, and it was as if I was underwater. I could see the surface, and hear people calling me to wake up. Pass me a tissue."

Charlie didn't think he'd seen Tom cry, not like this. "Don't tell me if you don't want to, lovey."

Tom blew his nose, one handed, then took a shuddery breath. "No. I want to. I kept listening for your voice, and then I remembered the bookshop and the shooting, and I thought maybe you weren't calling me because you were dead, and I didn't want to ..."

Charlie stroked Tom's hair and hugged him as hard as the bed and the tubes permitted. The story of what happened could wait.

FORTY-ONE
THURSDAY 1AM

The nurses asked Charlie to go in quiet voices and without the threat of calling security. He still didn't want to leave Tom, but on the promise that he could return anytime the next day, he got a cab back to the hotel and his clothes. He ordered pizza, and ate it sitting cross-legged on his bed, and when he couldn't face another slice, he leaned back and picked up the phone Murphy had given him.

"Hey, Brody, ready to tell me what's going on? Am I still a wanted man?"

"Warrant dropped. You're free and clear. As for what's going on, you know as much as I do."

Charlie growled. "Brody. Mate. You have lied to me since we met. Isn't there some old Chinese proverb about if you save someone's life, you're responsible for them forever? Well, you probably saved my life, so I think the responsible thing would be to tell me the truth."

There was a chuckle from Murphy's end of the phone. "Tomorrow. Because I am in my own bed for the first time in what feels like weeks."

"I don't want to know about your bed-hopping habits. You can meet Tom, and he can tell you about his encounter with Kaylan." Charlie ignored the spluttering, and ended the call.

THE NEXT MORNING, Charlie checked out of the hotel and headed back to the hospital, to find Tom sitting up in bed. He still looked as if he'd been run over by a train, and he was still attached to a drip and a selection of monitors. But the trajectory looked positive.

"If I am extremely good," he said to Charlie, after they had kissed. "I may be allowed to visit the bathroom to pee. Under supervision of course."

"And eat real food?"

"I think that's tomorrow's treat."

Charlie told Tom how he was no longer a wanted man, which meant explaining about having his clothes taken for forensic examination and the arrest warrant for Kaylan's murder.

"I should have kicked him harder last year," Tom said.

"He's dead though," Charlie said. "I can't think of a single nice thing to say about him, but he was only twenty." He held his hand up. "I know, Rico was only a kid, too. It's like Kaylan spread death and destruction everywhere he went. Dusty — the bookshop owner — and the other guy, killed because they were in the same room as Kaylan. And everyone who was there is going to remember it even if they weren't injured." He rubbed his hands over his eyes. "In other news, I've been spending your money and writing in your sketch book. Talking about your sketch book, I'd like to know when you drew some of those ... more *intimate* pictures."

They were laughing at the idea of Tom breaking off from

lovemaking to draw NSFW images of Charlie when Brody Murphy joined them, carrying what Charlie hoped was a bag of doughnuts. Charlie blushed and quickly shuffled the sketch-book back into the messenger bag.

"Sorry to interrupt," Murphy said, holding out his hand to Tom. "I'm Special Agent Brody Murphy, FBI, Quantico. My job is investigating allegations of corruption within law enforcement."

Which you could have mentioned from the start.

"Which I should probably have told you earlier," Murphy said to Charlie.

Charlie shrugged. Because he totally should have, but he was being honest now and that would have to do.

"You were after Mead and Bart all along? Not Dwyer?" Charlie asked, more for Tom's benefit than his own.

"The Bureau as a whole has an interest in Dwyer. Without going into too much detail, the relationship between the Sullys and Dwyer, and a possible Dwyer move into a particular vein of politics was setting off a few alarm bells. The decision to bring Kaylan Sully back from the UK seemed like a risky move, but perhaps a way of bringing some things out into the open."

"You didn't want the January sixth conspirators to get access to any more money or better cyberhackers? And you thought Dwyer and the Sullys were in with that crowd and that some of your people were helping them." Tom said.

Murphy just smiled.

"And my poor Charlie got dragged into your political mess because he wanted to know who killed Kaylan, even though Kaylan was a piece of shit who shot him and let his friend die?"

Murphy smiled again. "Charlie solved a domestic murder, yes. Probably two domestic murders. It looks likely that Sabrina Sully killed her husband. Let's not forget her other two victims either."

The silence following that admission was broken by a nurse coming to take Tom's blood pressure and check all the monitors and the drip.

"That fake serial-killer set-up in the flat we visited. Was that Mead and Bart?" Charlie asked when the nurse had gone.

"Probably. Forensic investigators are going over it. Bart might tell us. There are a lot of things Bart might tell us if he wants to avoid a very long sentence in a very unpleasant federal prison. Like who else in the Bureau they were working with, because there are more than just those two, but I didn't tell you that."

Murphy stood up. "It was nice to meet you," he said to Tom. "I've been asked to give you this. Only a copy, but you'll get the real thing in due course." He gave Tom an envelope.

Charlie stood up to see him out, and was surprised to be grabbed into a hug.

"It's been an experience," Murphy said. "Give me a call next time you visit the states." Then he bent down and handed Charlie the bag. "Your favourite, I think." And with that, he left.

"*Oh my fucking God,*" Tom said.

Charlie turned away from contemplating the doughnuts to see Tom staring at a piece of paper.

"*Kaylan fucking Sully left all his money to the art college.*" Tom thrust the paper at Charlie. It was a photocopy of what appeared to be a properly drawn up will. Leaving all Kaylan's worldly goods to Llanfair College of Art.

Charlie didn't know whether to laugh or cry at Kaylan's will. On one hand it would solve Tom's funding problems at a stroke. On the other, how much of the money was stolen? And on yet another hand, wouldn't it be better to deprive people like Sabrina Sully and Andrew Dwyer and spend the money on art instead? Could they just have the grandmother's inheritance, if it existed?

"We'll leave it to the lawyers," Tom concluded. "But if anyone thinks I'm naming even a broom cupboard after Kaylan Sully, they've got another think coming."

Charlie moved back into the flat, and spent his days sitting with Tom, who had left intensive care for an ordinary ward, disconnected from all his machines, though still subject to being poked and prodded. Tom and Charlie video-called the twins, Ann and Orianna, and Tom left a terse message for his parents saying that he would be returning to the UK soon.

"We would prefer that you didn't fly for another couple of weeks," his doctor told him on his discharge from hospital with a paper sack full of medication. "The absolute last thing you need is a blood clot."

"It's either sail home on the *Queen Mary* or stay in New York and do all the things we missed out on," Tom told Charlie. A phone call to Mal Kent bought Charlie two weeks unpaid leave, and they set out to see New York City, Tom with a walking stick, and Charlie with the messenger bag full of sketchbooks and pencils. The weather got warmer, and the city busier. Their attempts at tourism were often abandoned for days in Central Park with picnics, reading, sketching and quiet conversation.

Tom was easily tired, so one day Charlie left him in bed and went to try to find the homeless man who had helped him on the day of the drive-by shooting. He wasn't there, and there was no sign that he ever had been. There were a couple of chips missing from the steps he had hidden behind. The Dunkin' Donuts on the corner seemed to attract the homeless, the hearers of silent voices and the pushers of trolleys full of plastic bags. Charlie went in and asked if there was a homeless shelter nearby. The staff member shrugged, but his colleague said, yes, there was and gave Charlie an odd look to go with the directions. The shelter was in a run-down building across the street from a high-end bagel shop. Charlie found his way in and wasn't altogether surprised to see the man with dreadlocks who had told him not to ring the police.

"What do you want?" he demanded.

"I wanted to thank the guy who helped me when I was shot at," Charlie said. "But I can't find him."

"Moved on."

"Then I would like to make a donation to your work here," Charlie said. "Anonymously."

The man pushed a card across the counter. "Bank account details," he said.

Charlie got out his wallet. "Five hundred dollars. I'm sorry if I made your job harder that day," he said, picked up the card, smiled and left.

"Thanks," the man called after him.

Charlie wanted to remonstrate that not all police officers were the same, but he thought that if you were Black, and homeless, they probably were.

HE WAS SURPRISED to find Brody Murphy chatting with Tom in the living room when he got back.

"Hey, Charlie," Brody said, and gave him a hug.

"Have you come to arrest me, or is it Tom this time?" Charlie asked.

"Kaylan's mother died," Tom said.

"Poetic justice, I suppose," Charlie said, but he couldn't be happy that there had been yet another death. Sabrina and he shared exactly no opinions, but he remembered how she had stuck up for Kaylan when he had first rung her from Wales. "*I love my son, because that's what mothers do,*" she had said. Just another self-deception. When Murphy left, Charlie poured beers for himself and Tom and snuggled up to him on the sofa. The window was open, letting the sounds of the city below into the room, along with the scent of spring grass and outdoor grills.

"I look at your parents, Tom, and I see my own," he said. "None of them any happier with their sons than Sabrina Sully was happy with Kaylan. And all it does is add to the quantity of the world's misery and I've finished with it. I'm letting it go. My mother has a shitty life. My father is a drunk, and she's running a business she hates. But it's *her choice,* and I'm not taking responsibility for it any longer." Charlie felt the weight lift from his shoulders as he spoke. "Look at us. Last year I asked you if you were successful and you said yes. But it's never good enough, is it? You're not good enough for your folks. I'm not good enough for mine. I'm over being not good enough."

Tom's fingers tightened around his. "You're good enough for me. Better than good enough."

"You know what, Tom, you're right. I'm good at what I do, and I don't care if it's being a small-town cop. I'm successful dammit. I'm going to be a fantastic husband. I've been living one step removed from my own life. I let things happen instead of saying what I want. I wanted you from the first moment I saw you in the Rainbow, but I told myself there was something more important and got drunk instead. That's how I am. Always thinking there's something else I ought to be doing, and the only person who sees through it is you." He started to cry, putting his head on Tom's chest. He felt Tom stroke his hair.

"I think you're perfect, Charlie Rees."

SIX MONTHS LATER

It was cold and wet as Tom and Charlie trudged uphill through the woods. The scent of pine trees and damp earth was strong. Lichen glowed after the rain. At the top there was a magnificent view, or there would be if the clouds lifted. On a good day it was possible to see right across the valley to the mountains of Snowdonia rising beyond. Beyond the mountains was the sea and then Ireland, and beyond that, the Atlantic Ocean all the way to New York.

Tom reached for Charlie's hand, and found it slick with rain. He pulled Charlie toward him and they kissed, faces speckled with tiny drops of moisture. Their lips were warm, and Charlie smelled of sheep's wool from the new sweater he had bought from a craft stall on the market.

"It's still too warm, really," Charlie said. "But it's cooling down. Don't you feel it cooling down?"

"You can keep me warm," Tom said. He slipped his hands under the bottom of Charlie's new sweater, and he kissed Charlie's neck below his ear.

"You're tickling me," Charlie was laughing, but he didn't

move away. Tom's dick was obviously on board as Charlie pushed him against a tree and their kisses became deeper, tongues tangling. Charlie was hard too. They drew away to breathe and Charlie laughed again. "I can't get enough of you, Tomos Dylan," he said. "I even want to fuck you in the rain."

"I dreamt about this," Tom said. "This exact situation. You and me, in the rain, talking about fucking. Kissing against a tree."

"This is real."

"Is it though? It seemed real in my dream, only I couldn't wake up. That's how I knew it was a dream. I dreamed I was waking up and realised I was still dreaming. I'm not making any sense."

Charlie pulled Tom even closer, cupping his cheeks with wet hands. "Did I do this in your dream?" And kissed him again. "Were we getting married next week in your dream? Did we decide to abandon this soggy walk in your dream and go home so you could fuck me into the mattress and then I could do the same to you?"

"None of that," Tom said, "but it all sounds good."

"It's not a dream," Charlie said, the love bubbling up inside him making him feel weightless with elation. "Come with me and I'll prove it."

THE END

I hope you have enjoyed Charlie's New York adventure. If you have, I'd be delighted if you could leave a review wherever you review your books!

ACKNOWLEDGMENTS

This book was written during time of great personal upheaval, and there were times I thought it would never be finished. But, as always, friends went the extra mile to help, and it got done. So ... thanks are due to:

Lou for endless encouragement and nitting.

Glo, who more than anyone else, has given me the space and time to write, by doing the impossible with the Wayward Dog. And providing the ice-cream.

Bill and Austin for more encouragement and your calm assurance that I am now a proper writer .

JL Merrow and Kris Jacen for what can only be described as *emergency editing*.

Layla Ndn PA. Thanks!

Pixelstudio for the great covers.

The real A to Z (and Aubrey) who gave me the excuse for two amazing weeks holiday in NYC, a city I love, though don't know nearly as well as I'd like.

SF for keeping me sane.

To my many friends on social media. Social media gets a bad rep, but I have found lots of support and encouragement (as well as kitten pictures).

Above all, thanks to you, dear reader.

ABOUT THE AUTHOR

Ripley Hayes lives in West Wales, in a small town surrounded by green hills and ancient woodlands. She didn't take up writing fiction until she retired from a long career as a university lecturer and housing researcher. Since then, she has done little else, to the despair of her friends and dog. Her books are the kinds of books she likes to read: mysteries with wickedness but not too much blood, and romance with real people who make mistakes, all set in interesting places.

When she's not writing, Ripley likes to read, travel, knit, and eat chocolate, ideally all at once.

Ripley has a website, and a newsletter.

You can also contact her on Facebook at Ripley Hayes & Co.

ALSO BY RIPLEY HAYES

Printed in Great Britain
by Amazon

37025886R00118